THE FAINT-HEARTED BOLSHEVIK

THE FAINT-HEARTED BOLSHEVIK

LORENZO SILVA

Translated from the Spanish by
Nick Caistor and Isabelle Kaufeler

Hispabooks Publishing, S. L.
Madrid, Spain
www.hispabooks.com

Originally published in Spain as *La flaqueza del bolchevique* by Destino, 1997
First published in English by Hispabooks, 2013

A CIP record for this book is available from the British Library

ISBN 978-84-940948-2-8 (trade paperback)
ISBN 978-84-940948-3-5 (ebook)
Legal Deposit: M-22800-2013

To my grandfathers Lorenzo and Manuel,
in memoriam

Of their sweet deaths are sweetest odours made.

SHAKESPEARE, *Sonnets,* LIV

Sooner murder an infant in its cradle than nurse unacted desires.

BLAKE, *Proverbs of Hell*

THIRTEEN (OR FIFTEEN) YEARS LATER

Note to the 2010 Spanish edition

This book, which first saw the light of day in February 1997, was written during the spring and summer of 1995. Therefore, depending on how you look at it, I am writing this note thirteen or fifteen years later. A long time for a novel, under normal conditions; long enough not to expect a new edition.

The fact that this new edition exists is due to the sustained support of its publishers (who, as far as I can remember, have not let a single year go by since its publication without reprinting it) and, above all, thanks to the goodwill of very diverse and generous readers for whom these lines are intended as an expression of my gratitude. Firstly, no small thanks are due to the members of the reading panel and jury of the Premio Nadal 1997, for which I was a finalist. A special mention to Rosa Regàs, Pere Gimferrer, Jorge Semprún, Andreu Teixidor and Antoni Vilanova, and also to Elena Lauroba and Eduardo Gonzalo.

I should also mention those other special readers, members of the team who adapted the novel for the film version directed by Manuel Martín Cuenca and produced by José Antonio Romero. I would also like to thank all the teachers who recommended the book to their students, both at secondary school and university, to my initial surprise and even alarm, given the nature of the story, which some might consider scandalous. I was also afraid the story might evoke too much of a sense of loss to interest those who, still in the first flush of youth, were too young to have experienced something similar. I extend my thanks to those young people for interpreting my characters in a different way, and for making them their own in accordance with their own codes of understanding that I could never have imagined.

But there were many others. In particular, I want to thank the readers who are well acquainted with the world to which the protagonist belongs and which he describes here and there in the book, because they have lived there too. That world where, in another time, investment bankers like our protagonist were the chosen ones: clever and influential young men, marking the course of history with their tricks and bright ideas until it left them behind and plunged them into a state of bewilderment that still overwhelms them (and which is shared by the rest of us, as victims of the collapse of their house of cards). The world of the company where, as described in certain passages of the novel, the workers were divided into different castes, subject to blatant inequalities that time has not corrected, but reinforced. So much so that the book is used by some professors of Labor Law as a reference point to explain the current system of labor relations in Spain. That the book remains relevant in this respect, and to such a degree, is something the author can only regret.

As for the rest, I am naturally delighted. I'm pleased that, in spite of the crude nature of his narrative, which is retained in this new edition apart from the odd correction, this poor Bolshevik has found and continues to find companions on his journey. Not only in his original language, but also in others as dear to the author as Russian, French or Czech. This makes it possible for his grueling and ill-timed love story (in the end what is left to us, if not love?) to survive beyond the moment of adversity in which it arose and had to be hurriedly set down. Perhaps his prayers have been heard after all. We mortals can ask no more of the gods.

El Prat de Llobregat,
16 December 2009

It was Monday and, like every Monday, my soul felt like a dead weight down there, just below my nut sack. One afternoon I imagined my soul as a third ball hanging there, about as much use to me as the other two. Ever since, when it's Monday and my soul feels like a dead weight, when it's any other day and my soul feels like a dead weight, even when I don't know what day it is and my soul feels like a dead weight, I feel this bulk and this heaviness down below, bulging against the stretch fabric of my underpants.

I haven't always been someone with his soul between his balls. For years I didn't even use four letter words, and for many years I even used a varied and refined vocabulary. Now I've decided you don't need more than five hundred or so words to get through life and that four letter words are the most appropriate. It's not that I've never got beyond this point, but that this is where I've ended up. Lots of losers get stuck where I am right now very early on in their lives and stay here forever. I've arrived here via a number of other places along the way, some of which smelled much better, although it never lasted long. It might seem as though I'd have been better off if, right from the start, I'd been one of those losers who've never noticed what happens around them or who have never been anywhere that smelled better. I couldn't agree more. If I'd been a loser all my life I would be satisfied now, rather than remembering that it was a Monday that day, and that my soul felt like a dead weight inside my underpants.

The Monday I am remembering began with the same shit as every Monday. There were five dickheads on the radio talking about what another five dickheads had said, so that the next day another five dickheads (some of them the same as the previous day) could talk about what these five dickheads had said and so on to infinity, a mishmash of teams of five dickheads. As my tolerance for bullshit has diminished over the years, I put a tape in the car cassette player and it turned out to be one I'd made years ago of that old fart Bach. Although I'd erased them all, recording better music over them, sometimes fragments of his infuriating cantatas (they're all about the same thing, and all sound the same) sneak in. I fast forwarded the tape a bit and found "Breaking the Law" by Judas Priest. I left it on, not because I like those Judas dudes—in fact, I think they are a bunch of louts who've never had a single original thought in their life—but because they make a hell of a noise and that stops me thinking. Most of all, I was trying to escape from what was weighing so heavily on my soul, which was the same thing as always: it was Monday (fucking Monday), it was early (fucking early), I was in the car (fucking car), stuck in a traffic jam (fucking traffic jam), undecided as to whether to place my tie under or over the seatbelt (fucking seatbelt, fucking tie); I was on my way to work, where, in exchange for wasting my days they give me money to buy food and pay my rent and my car and my tie and my radio and the CDs I use to make tapes of Judas Priest (fucking work, fucking days, fucking money, fucking food, fucking apartment, etc.). And then, as usual, a cop holding up traffic at the Plaza de Cibeles so that the cars coming down Calle de Alcalá could get through and to hell with those of us coming up Paseo del Prado (fucking cop).

It's easy for me to remember what I was thinking of, because I do it often and I know it by heart. The stuff about the traffic cop too, because he does the exact same thing every morning. As for Bach and Judas Priest—and here is where it all starts—I remember them clearly because just as I found "Breaking the Law", the car in front of me braked sharply and, distracted by the music, I slammed it at thirteen miles an hour, which is nothing in terms of covering the ten miles I drive every morning, but more than enough to crash one car into another.

At that moment all hell broke loose, and hell it was, in the following order: this Chanel-clad bitch gets out of the car in front, comes over and starts calling me son of a bitch, bastard, and countless other things not at all in keeping with her classy outfit; the prick of a traffic cop's eyes almost fall out of his head, and without bothering to take the whistle out of his mouth he comes over to the scene of the accident, eager to join the fun and games; the drivers behind us who start blasting their horns to see if they can drive me crazy once and for all; the seatbelt refuses to obey me as I jerk it in an attempt to unbuckle it because I must be pulling a bit harder than the manufacturer considers appropriate; the boys in the Judas Priest band who seem set on trashing their drums, their bass and all their guitars.

By the time I finally managed to free myself from the seatbelt and get out of the car, the Chanel-clad bitch and the cop had clearly become close allies.

"First things first: move the car out of here. Can't you see you're blocking traffic?" the cop spat at me as soon as I stuck my head out the window.

"It would help if she moved hers first," I answered, like a complete idiot. "I'm stuck up her rear end."

"Did you hear the son of a bitch?" the woman raged. "Why don't you go and stick your damn car up your fucking mother's ass?"

"Sure, great idea. But if you don't move your car, I can't move mine either, and the officer here won't be able to get the traffic moving, which is what he wants to do."

"Ma'am," the cop added, "if you cooperate with me I'm sure we can solve this very quickly."

The woman moved her car and I moved mine, while the cop redirected the motherfuckers who drove past us, laughing at the crash. I looked for the car registration papers, the insurance documents and a ballpoint and found everything except the ballpoint. I didn't much like the idea of asking the woman or the cop for a pen, but the funny thing about user-friendly, European accident forms is that they are printed on carbonless paper and you know just where you can stick your Mont Blanc Meiserstück when your have to fill one in. Resigned to my fate, I got out to face what was coming. The woman was still insulting me and when she saw me she barked:

"So, you idiot, did you manage to con someone into insuring you?"

"If the officer weren't here you wouldn't call me an idiot."

"Why? What would you do if the officer weren't here?"

I'd kick you in the cunt until my leg got tired, I thought, but I said, "I'd probably drive off and leave you howling at the moon."

"Don't be stupid. As if they wouldn't track you down."

"Of course they would. But you're not hurt. I wouldn't go to jail. I'd give the police my insurance details and save myself the pleasure of this conversation."

At that point the cop came back over to where we were standing. He opened proceedings with a stupid question: "Ok people, what happened?"

"I was driving along, minding my own business. I braked because the lights changed and then he comes and crashes into me from behind."

"I didn't do it for fun," I joked. "I was distracted by the music. If I'd seen her I wouldn't have crashed into her from behind."

"Officer, I demand you stop this moron laughing. This is hardly a laughing matter."

"Listen, you two, cool it. Both of you, calm down."

"I've calmed down now, sir."

"I should hope so, it was his fault."

"But of course it was my fault. Why don't we fill in the forms first and then you can summon the firing squad?"

"Driver's license and vehicle registration papers."

I gave the documents to the cop. He was clearly disappointed not to be able to fine me for leaving them at home or forgetting to renew my license, which was the most he would have been able to do as a result of his brilliant check. Meanwhile Judas continued blasting from my car.

"Can't you turn that damn music off?"

"Lady, I have treated you with respect. And I haven't bitched about the music you listen to."

"You could at least have rolled up the window."

"The window is jammed. This is as far as it goes. I'll try and make sure my car is in good condition next time."

"This guy's a real son of a bitch, plus he's getting a kick out of this."

"Officer, I can see that you're busy, but do I have to put up with this lady hurling insults at me all the time?"

"I said cool it, you two. Show me your proof of insurance and fill out the forms, please."

The cop gave me back my papers disgruntled at not being able to throw the book at me. Addressing the woman, he said, "I'll need to see your driver's license too."

Since sometimes I just don't know when to keep my mouth shut, I asked: "Aren't you going to ask her for her car papers too?"

"She hasn't broken the law, sir."

"And me, what have I done?"

"You ran a red light."

"If that's so, what makes you think that because I ran a red light I don't have my driver's license with me? It seems more likely to be the opposite to me. If I'm planning to crash into a car driven by a hysterical woman in front of an officer while running a red light, I'd be better off having all my papers in order. Most likely she's the one who doesn't have her papers in order. She didn't know I was going to crash into her."

"Hysterical woman. Holy fucking shit."

"Don't make things more difficult," said the cop.

"What I don't understand is why you insist on harassing innocent people. If we were on a vacant lot and you were on your own and I had four buddies with me carrying baseball bats, you wouldn't ask me for anything."

"Don't kick up a fuss, come on."

"Don't pay any attention to him, officer. He must have had some sort of fit," remarked the woman, suddenly calm.

At that point I stopped to look at her. She was about thirty-five, bottle blonde, scrawny, with a sun-bed tan. She was wearing a pair of sunglasses three or four times the size of her face, and her shirt buttons were undone far enough for the pale fabric to contrast with her baked skin and for men to see her boobs. And, presumably so that she could get angry when that happened, she wore a gold crucifix nestling in her cleavage. She also wore lots of rings and bracelets and her nails looked like they'd never scratched one of those greasy crusts resistant even to the best detergent for ceramic cooktops.

"What are you're staring at?" she barked again.

"I must ask you to cooperate," the cop insisted.

There are a million cars in this fucking city and I have to go and crash into this bitch, I thought. Maybe that meant something. In any case, it didn't seem the right moment to rack my brains, so I decided to do as the cop said.

"Do you have a pen?" I asked. "It's for the carbonless paper" and I pulled the cap off my Mont Blanc to show how useless it was.

The cop lent me a ballpoint and I wrote my address and all the other details you have to fill in on the form. I admitted responsibility for the whole mess and started to draw a diagram of the accident. Then I stopped. Although the drawing was not complicated, it occurred to me she might have seen things differently.

"You do the drawing if you like. I've already admitted it was my fault."

The woman took out a small silver Dupont ballpoint and, somewhat irritated at having to do it herself, wrote down her details and carelessly finished off my diagram. The cop checked the information and copied some of them onto a small printed form he made us both sign. Incidentally, he looked carefully at my license plate before writing the number down. He had already looked at it once when I had given him the car papers. Once he had finished he tore off the two copies of the form and gave us one each.

"Very well. You can go," he said to the woman.

"You don't need to tell me twice. Goodbye and good riddance," the latter directed at me.

"Why can't I go?"

"I need to issue the fine."

"Listen, officer. If I've done something wrong, God has already punished me enough. Why rub it in by adding a fine on top?"

"It's my duty. And yours is to drive more carefully."

The bitch in the Chanel suit had already got into her car, one of those white convertibles that bitches like her always drive, and I had to watch as she adjusted the rear-view mirror, checked her hair and fluffed it up, while the fucking cop pissed me off and gleefully earned his damn salary, that, for better or for worse, is all what we losers get, whether it's because we've always been losers or because we've ended up being that way.

By the time I climbed back into my car I'd wasted twenty minutes and the early start I'd made so that the traffic jam I would get stuck in wasn't the usual eight-thirty-Monday-morning damn traffic jam. By now it was eight-thirty and not only was I stuck in the middle of the damn traffic jam but I was going to be late, which would make this Monday even more Mondayish and my soul between my balls weigh twice as much as it had done up till then. That was when I realized that the name and address of the bitch in the Chanel suit were in the folder with my insurance documents. Around me, everyone was honking their horns, taxi drivers were sneaking past me, and the traffic hadn't moved a damn inch. I opened the folder and read the whore's name: Sonsoles. And the first half of her surname: López-Díaz. And the second half: García-Navarro. Or, rather, Sonsoles López García, who had deemed it beneath her to be known as López García and who had rescued her grandmothers from oblivion by adding their last names to hers. Or her father had done it, or her father's father, which would have been even worse. From the address she had written on the form, I worked out that she lived in the area around the church of Los Jerónimos, next to the Prado Museum. When I was a sensitive fool I used to like that neighborhood. It's quiet at night and during the day the only bother, if any, are the hordes of japs taken by coach to gawp at the paintings.

While I got on with my daily grind, I started thinking. It occurred to me that Sonsoles López García might be a possibility of avoiding a lingering death by boredom. Now, I don't believe in fate: I think almost everything happens because one insists on making it happen, sometimes thanks to more than a little effort, it's true, but that doesn't make one less responsible or less of an idiot. I had crashed into that Sonsoles slut that morning in a really stupid way and certainly without the slightest intention of doing so. Yet something had put her there in front of me, and I had crashed into her. For the time being I had only dented my car, which was a shame, but who knew if I couldn't get something good out of this episode. And by something good I was thinking of having some fun: not too much, after all, if I'd thought at the time that life could be really fun, I wouldn't have buried Mozart as well under the blazing guitars of Judas Priest (and Kreator and 77 Fucking Bastards and Blame It On Your Dirty Sister). While my dented car clanked up the Paseo de la Castellana, an evil plan was taking shape in my head. And I laughed to myself, I swear I laughed as if someone had told me the best joke I'd ever heard in my life.

And that is the inexplicable way that Sonsoles came into my pathetic life and how, by playing around like a fool, I managed to turn a simple traffic accident into a hell of a downfall.

Now that I come to think about it, it's weird that everything started with the car. Modern man is totally dependent on machines, and of all the machines the one that leaves modern man drooling is the fucking car. Modern man spends hours on his car, he gets into debt to buy it, he doesn't sleep if it makes a strange noise or if it sticks when he's changing gear. Many men don't spend as much time with their families as they do with their cars; they spend less money on their families than on their cars, and they don't give a damn if one of their kids has a fever, which in the case of a child is about the same as the car breaking down, and decidedly more serious than any squeaking noise coming from the car's shock absorbers.

When his luck improves, a modern man buys himself a car. If more than four or five years have passed since he bought the last one and he hasn't got a new one, his fellow modern men consider him a bit of a loser. One of the few reasons why a modern man might kill another is because the latter has blocked his way. One of the few reasons why a modern man under thirty years of age might stop paying into Social Security is because of a traffic accident.

Personally, my first car was very important to me because at the time I had X pesetas and the car cost me X plus 500,000 pesetas. Also, because the motherfucker's fuel injection system didn't work very well and every other day you could find me at the garage struggling to put up with some idiot who insisted that gas here in Spain was very dirty, not like the stuff they had in Germany, which was what they always told me because they didn't have the imagination to think up a more convincing piece of nonsense.

The second car was less important to me, because by that time I had more money, and because the fuel injection system was just as God had intended fuel injection systems to be: resistant to any type of dirt contained in the fuel in the country where the car was sold.

The third, which is the one I drove into Sonsoles' rear end, didn't really matter to me. Or at least that's what I thought. If I'm not mistaken, I bought it because it was the cheapest one available that had air conditioning and enough power for me to overtake a truck without risking my life.

However, one night when I had an upset stomach, I discovered that my bowels had something in common with my car's, something so weird it was almost alarming: the smell of my farts under the sheets was identical to the smell of unleaded fuel once it had been burnt up by my car' s engine and had passed through its catalytic convertor. I'd only recently bought it, and I'd spent weeks trying to figure out what the stench flooding my garage every day reminded me of. Although it has nothing at all to do with this story, I think that was the night I decided to add to my list of carefully hidden personality traits that of enemy of ecology.

I also hate pedagogy, liberal capitalism and sports. I don't know why everything that tries, or claims to try, to improve people's lives sooner or later ends up ruining them.

Sonsoles López García had taken a precaution she knew would not affect the paperwork needed for the repair of her hideous convertible, and the result was that I had to work a bit harder. She had merely barred with a line the box designated for the telephone number of the driver of vehicle B. And I could tell it had been done with malicious intent because the line went up quite a bit at the end. Back in the days when I used to read things other than work stuff and my utility bills, I once read a book on graphology. It said that people whose signature slants upwards at the end are either the enthusiastic sort or pretty bad-tempered. It didn't seem to me that Sonsoles López García was easily enthused, except when she went to buy gold trinkets to put around her wrists or on her fingers or to hang between her tits. I'm not an enthusiastic person either and my signature slants up at almost thirty degrees.

Someone should have told Sonsoles that not giving your telephone number is just fucking stupid when you give your address. Sooner or later the telephone number can be found. And in Sonsoles' case, it was extraordinarily easy. As soon as my butt touched the chair in my office, the first thing I did was dial 003 for information.

"Your call will be served by operator eight … four … nine," the telephone company computer stuttered. "Good morning, Information" a human being took over. A female human being, to be more precise.

"Good morning. I'd like the telephone number for Señorita Sonsoles López-Díaz. Her surname's double-barrelled. She lives on Calle Moreto, at number 46."

"There's no one by that name, sir."

"Is there anyone else by the last name López-Díaz or López at that address?"

"I can't give you that information, sir."

"Okay, thanks, Mata Hari."

I hung up and dialled again.

"Your call will be served by operator seven … three … one." This time I got a man. "Good morning, Information Department."

"Good morning. I'd like the telephone number for Señor López-Díaz."

"You've got to be kidding. I'm not Colombo," joked the operator.

"It's not that difficult. He lives at 46 Calle Moreto."

There was the sound of a computer keyboard. A second later the operator was back.

"Armando López-Díaz. Have a pen and paper ready."

The voice of the other computer, the one that greeted you and clicked on the numbers, dictated a telephone number. If I hadn't hung up it would have kept dictating numbers to me until every last one of my teeth fell out.

I dialled the seven digits. A young woman answered.

"Hello?"

"Hello. Who's that speaking?"

"Lucía."

"Ah. I'd like to speak to Sonsoles."

"She's out."

"When will she be back?"

"Who are you?"

"Antonio. I work with Don Armando."

"And why do you want to talk to Sonsoles?"

It was obvious that I had cleared the first hurdle. I'd planned to amuse myself for longer, but I threw myself into the next one, one I knew she wouldn't fall for:

"You see, I met Sonsoles about a month ago. She came back to my place, had a bit much to drink, and, well, you know how these things happen … I wanted to use a condom because I'm bisexual and some of my friends sleep around, but she wouldn't let me. Now I've had a blood test and according to the results … "

"That's not funny, you jerk."

"Don't hang up on me, this is important for your sister."

"She's not my sister. I work here."

"It doesn't matter, she needs to know anyway."

"To know what? You've got AIDS, right? And I'm the Empress of Iran."

"Not exactly."

"What then?"

"Look, now I think about it, it's a very delicate matter. I'm going to give you my phone number. Tell her to call me."

I took out my collection of carefully chosen telephone numbers and after wavering between the Archbishopric of

Madrid-Alcalá and the Ministry for Social Affairs, I gave her the number for the police station in Tetuán.

"If you think I'm going to take down that number you've got another thing coming," she replied.

"Write it down and give it to her. What could happen?"

"They might fire me, for starters."

"Tell her I'm a prank caller. You'll see how seriously she takes it."

"Fine, tell me the number again. That way we'll have something to give the police."

I repeated it.

"And please, don't let her husband find out," I snivelled.

"She doesn't have a husband. Goodbye, you jerk."

Lucía slammed the phone down on me, as they say in American detective novels, which is to say I had the phone pressed to my ear when she hung up, opening a couple of cracks in my eardrum.

Whether it was a stroke of luck or because I'm a fucking genius, that brief phone call had helped me confirm a number of things. Sonsoles was single. She lived with her father, a certain Don Armando who must be quite a big shot and who could very well have a colleague named Antonio, and someone called Lucía as a maid, who wasn't in the least intimidated by talk of bisexuals and venereal diseases.

That morning I had more than enough work to keep me busy, things I had left half-finished on Friday night and others I'd been putting off but couldn't put off any longer without my boss calling to ask who did I think I was and being unable to tell him the truth. Since I get pissed off when I have to lie unless I'm doing it for fun, I plunged back into my work and forgot about Sonsoles until that night. I've often found that leaving everything until the last minute is the most effective way of working. Things get done where there's no choice but to do them, and since there's no choice but to do them, they get done one after the other, quickly and without thought. When the god Yahweh told Adam he'd have to slave away to avoid dying of hunger and that He'd put a stop to any more raids on the fruit trees, He didn't think he was screwing Adam over because he was incapable of wielding a hoe, or because wielding a hoe would be an unsustainable effort for him. He knew he was screwing him over because His creature Adam was a bum who would spend the whole time he was hoeing thinking what a hardship it was. The bad thing about working isn't the work per se, but the thought that you're working. Just thinking is fine, just working is less good, but thinking and working at the same time is worse than shooting yourself in the head. That's why the wisest of the Greeks jerked off with both hands while that idiot Plato used his to write down everything he saw.

That night I left the Bank early, early meaning nine o'clock p.m. There were still another ten or fifteen cocksuckers just like me at work on my floor, except they had nothing to do once they left the office and so they would stay there until they were kicked out. One day I'll tell you about how things are run at the damn office, which is sort of like an ant-hill but even more frantic. You either have to laugh or cry, depending on how you feel that day and how fucking angry you are at being a member of the cocksucking ant brigade.

As I picked up my car I remembered I'd have to take it to the garage to have a nose job the next day. I immediately set off in the direction of the Paseo del Prado. I parked where I used to when I used to hang around that area, just where the Ritz Hotel keeps its garbage cans. Although there's always someone shooting up in the phone booth, the hotel staff are more or less alert. I don't think they'd do anything at all if they saw someone robbing a car, except wishing it was over as soon as possible, but although junkies aren't at all worried about having an audience, thieves, on the other hand, feel more at ease when no-one's watching. These are the types of things one should be aware of. Since I wear decent clothes and earn a good salary and own things that can be stolen, I try to understand the habits of the have-nots. I know it sounds better to say you really care about the underprivileged and ethnic minorities and that you wouldn't mind sharing what you have with them, but it would be like a kick in the balls to anyone if such a person relieved you of belongings you weren't planning to share as yet.

I went into the phone booth, careful not to step on the syringes, and I didn't hold the phone too close to my ear. The mouthpiece stank of cigarettes and it wasn't easy to hold it close to your mouth even if you wanted to. I put in two hundred pesetas, dialled Sonsoles' number, and prepared myself to make the most of whoever might answer the phone.

"Yes," muttered an older woman. The weaker flank. Plan A.

"Good evening. Is this the home of Don Armando López-Díaz?"

"Yes. Who is calling?"

"I'm calling from the IRS."

"From where?"

"From the Inland Revenue Service. Is Señor López-Díaz there?"

"Yes. One moment, please."

Though Sonsoles' mother had covered the mouthpiece with her hand, I heard a series of whispers slipping through her fingers that ended in a gruff, manly *ahem*.

"Armando López-Díaz. To whom am I speaking?"

"Eduardo Gutiérrez, tax inspector. I am so sorry to be calling so late, Señor López-Díaz. We call in the evening because it's easier to reach tax-payers at home."

"Is something wrong? I declare all my earnings scrupulously."

Armando López-Díaz's voice quivered slightly as he lied.

"It's just routine. The computer has selected you as part of the Wealth Tax inspection. I'd like to know when you could have the paperwork ready to make a formal declaration."

"The paperwork … "

"For the last five years. All the paperwork relating to your tax returns."

"Oh, well, of course."

"And your answer?"

"Well … I need a couple of days to get the paperwork in order."

"Absolutely, and you are self employed, if my notes are not mistaken?"

"Yes. I'm a freelance architect."

"Exactly. And you use self-assessment."

"Yes, I think so. Yes."

Having discovered through sheer luck that Armando López-Díaz was a professional, it was easy as pie to figure out he had chosen the option that would allow him to deduct certain expenses, a taxi here, a telephone bill there, a rental car, claiming them as professional expenses. Until a tax inspector came along and forced him to get his act together. And there was another small disadvantage: he had to keep accounts.

"You'll also need to have all your accounts up-to-date."

"Of course, yes."

I was having the time of my life making Armando sweat. But I'm the impatient sort, and that wasn't what I really wanted to do.

"There's one more thing, Don Armando."

"Yes?" he asked, so faintly I could barely hear him.

"You have a daughter. Sonsoles López-Díaz García-Navarro."

"Yes. Why?"

"I believe she lives with you?"

"She's not here at the moment. I don't understand what … "

"And she's single."

"But what does that matter to the tax office?"

"Your daughter doesn't work, is that correct?"

"Yes, she does."

I let a couple of seconds of silence pass so that Don Armando would get anxious and be even less on the ball.

"That can't be the case, Don Armando. She doesn't have any income declared under her personal tax number. Is it possible she's being paid under the table?"

"Under the table? What are you saying? My daughter works for the Ministry of Industry. She's a Commercial Accountant for the Government." I could clearly hear the damn capital letters civil servants and the parents of civil servants always use.

"At the Ministry of Industry? That can't be true. In Madrid?"

"At the Ministry itself. Listen, what the hell is going on?"

"There's clearly something wrong. Please forgive me, Señor López-Díaz. We're going to have to verify all your daughter's information."

Armando's brain was creaking. It happens with most pompous asses. Their mind moves about as fast as a pregnant tortoise.

"I was under the impression that it was me you were after?" he tried to get himself together.

"And your daughter too. You've both been selected. There're no further complications as far as you're concerned because we do have your tax returns. You show me the supporting paperwork and your books, we compare them, and we stop bugging you. If everything's in order in half an hour we'll sign the form saying we've checked them and they match. As far as your daughter is concerned, according to the computer she hasn't paid any taxes. No tax returns, no deductions from her salary."

"That can't be true."

"If she works at the Ministry it's very strange that her income isn't showing up on the system. You wouldn't be covering up for her, would you?"

"For Heaven's sake. Why would I lie to you? If there's a mistake on the computer system you'll have to correct it."

"Fine. I'll tell you what we'll do. Tell your daughter to call this number at nine o'clock tomorrow morning. She'll need to give her name and say that she was selected on this month's list. Take note of the number."

I gave him the number for the Association of Marxist Lesbians and repeated it for him. Armando wrote it down, then assured me yet again in a barely audible voice like a little boy who never sticks his tongue out at the teacher:

"I'm sure there must be some mistake, take my word for it."

"We'll get to the bottom of this. Don't worry. With regard to your inspection, would next Monday suit?"

"Yes, that's fine."

"I'll send you the summons first thing tomorrow. Thank you for everything and good night."

"G ..."

This time it was me who slammed the phone down on one of the members of the López-Díaz household. As I got in the car I thought about how Sonsoles' poor father wouldn't sleep a wink that night and I didn't give even half a shit. As for Sonsoles herself, as well as filling in what I knew about her, I was confident I could cause her some trouble of the kind that really annoyed her.

On my way home, an unfortunate thought crossed my mind. Until now I hadn't done more than play a couple of pranks, nothing that had amused me as much as I'd hoped. My restlessness stayed with me after that, even while I sat in my living room cutting up the sleaziest images from a magazine full of naked men to send a collage to Sonsoles at the Ministry of Industry. That was child's play. Either I had to move on to the serious bit as soon as possible, or quit messing about. I would have to make an effort in the beginning, it must be said, but being bored was even worse. Since I've turned thirty, when I'm really bored I get violent, and I'm filled with a terrible urge to head-butt the television. That's something to be avoided since I need my head for work and I don't earn enough to buy a new TV set every day.

The television itself is not what matters, because almost everything they show is nonsense for mental midgets, which, by the way, means that everyone who doesn't receive any other form of education, in other words almost everyone, becomes a little bit more retarded every day. On the other hand they do broadcast women's ice-skating and gymnastics championships (both artistic and rhythmic) on television. I'm not that interested in ice-skating or gymnastics, but female skaters and gymnasts are one of the few things in life which justify my getting out of bed each day.

I woke up at the crack of dawn in a sweat and with my heart pounding. I tried to calm down and go back to sleep, but it was impossible. I got up and made myself a cup of lime blossom tea. Although this made me feel better, it wasn't enough. I put on my tracksuit and went out in the car. I drove along the M-30 motorway for a while. The M-40 has better bends and you can drive faster, but it has the disadvantage of being kept under surveillance by the Guardia Civil. Try any funny business and a guy on a motorcycle trained to hunt down hot rods starts breathing down your neck and they give you a fine that leaves you speechless. The M-30 is monitored by the Local Police, and either they don't have such good bikers or they only show them off during special events. The worst that can happen is they take your picture and send a fine to your house. I've got a hundred and seventy eight fines from the Local Police at home, all expired after they failed to deal with my objections appropriately. It's so easy to avoid paying fines that I ought to set up a consultancy service. Obviously one of these days they'll either learn or change the law, and then I'll have to buy a Scalextric.

When I got tired of putting the pedal to the metal I took the next exit and looked for a phone booth. I dialled Sonsoles' number. It rang six times, then after an impressive crack as if whoever had picked up the receiver had immediately dropped it, I heard Armando say, "Yes? Who is this?"

"Sonsoles," I whispered.

"Who is it?"

"Sonsoles," I whispered again.

"Go fuck yourself, you son of a bitch," and he hung up.

I repeated the process.

"Who the hell are you?" It was Armando again.

"Sonsoles," I whispered again.

He hung up. I waited ten minutes and rang again. This time it only rang twice.

"Who are you, you bastard?" trilled Sonsoles' unmistakeable voice.

I panted at some length. She remained silent until I stopped.

"Oooh, how dirty. Am I supposed to be scared?" she laughed.

She was right. That was a bit unoriginal. I took out a handkerchief and covered the mouthpiece. I put on a deep voice.

"Hello, Sonsoles. You don't know me, but I see you every day. I've been obsessed with you for weeks."

"Of course. And you want to ask me out on a date, or for me to tell you whether or not I'm wearing panties."

"I'm not that kind of man."

"So you think you're a man, do you?"

"More or less."

"More or less?"

"Do you know what I really want, Sonsoles?"

"I'm dying to find out."

"I want to tear out your liver and eat it fried. I'll feed your heart to my dog and I'll preserve the rest of you so that my monkey can have some fun with that and stops jerking off. In the meanwhile, I'll always be there, sweetie. Watch your back."

"I'm going to call the police right now." Sonsoles had stopped laughing.

"And what're you going to tell them? You don't have anything on me. I'm in a phone booth and you don't know who I am. Do you have any idea how many cases like this they file away every day? They'll wait until I really do something to you."

"I know who you are."

"Don't waste your time."

"You're a piece of shit."

"Of course I am. By the way, my monkey sends his love. He's looking forward to meeting you."

I hung up on her. That was more than enough for one night. What I'd done made me feel slightly disgusted with myself, of course, but I noticed that I'd relaxed considerably. There was a time when I hardly ever did that sort of sick prank, and thought that those who did were slimy buggers in a state of permanent anxiety and who wanted to kill themselves after every misdeed. However, now that I've become a pervert I've realized that when you give vent to your basic instincts you don't feel guilty, but empty, which is the only way a pervert can feel at peace with himself. When you go and do something disgusting, it's over and done with. The problem is when you stop halfway, because then the itch becomes unbearable.

That night, for example, I got home, went to bed and slept like a log. When I woke up, I saw that I had dribbled all over the pillow. Although Freud may not have written about it, preferring to waste his time on debatable subtleties, a dribble-filled sleep can only be a happy sleep.

The fucking office. Impressions of a victim:

At present, due to the inevitable upheavals as the millennium draws to a close, three very different castes coexist within the world of work.

First there are those, about thirty per cent or more of the workforce, who have been there forever and have stable positions in a well-established company and therefore, subsidised in some way or another. These companies are more common than you might think and no doubt also more common than suits those who don't enjoy their benefits. Thanks to their influential and seconded trade-union officials, these people haven't yet left the golden days when labor contracts were awesome. The days when they gave you a bonus after you'd spent X number of years with the company, when you went out for lunch at noon, you could have a leisurely cup of coffee in the morning, and when September came round everyone would get a bonus that was juicy enough to buy everything the kids needed to go back to school and with the rest you could go out for a night on the town, and finish off with a cigar and after dinner drinks. Naturally, the new model of labor relations tries to discourage such employees, but it would take an earthquake to unsettle them, and even then I'm not convinced they wouldn't think that earthquakes only upset staff on temporary contracts. They know that the worst that can happen to them is to get a golden handshake at the expense of young people's salaries, and then, nicely fattened up and pockets full of cash, they'll be sent home to wallow in all kinds of vices. This proceeding is what is most commonly known as early retirement. While they wait for the appropriate birthday or their turn, these buddhas while away their clearly defined eight hours a day ticking off days on the calendar and boxes on their betting slips or lottery tickets. They regularly suffer from all sorts of illnesses and injuries: flu (a fortnight off), hay fever in the spring (ten days off), a summer cold (eight days at home) and they always fracture a minor bone out jogging on the last day of their summer holidays (another three weeks off). Every couple of years they have to have a sebaceous cyst removed (a month off) and break a major bone skiing (two months off). And as all this still leaves more time in the office than is desirable, they won't give up a single long weekend.

Truth be told, among those who enjoy this blessed impunity, there are a few morons who work because they either have principles or because they feel a sort of religious calling to do so well. Of course they are everybody's laughing stock. Bear in mind that you have to be fool to have principles when no one else does (if ministers steal, they shouldn't expect anything different of me, according to ninety-five per cent of people participating in the latest surveys). And those with a vocation are by far the most ridiculed (more than ninety-nine per cent of respondents categorically declared that a vocation should only be expected from the motherfuckers who reap the benefits from it). So please forgive me if in this brief analysis I omit any further mention of this anomalous group so categorically condemned by popular wisdom.

Of the remaining seventy per cent, four fifths are crummy two-bit temps. Let's get this straight: I don't mean they have short-term contracts, but rather that they can be fired according to their employer's whims. In such incidences, the firing of a permanent employee is nothing more than a tacitly agreed failure to renew a contract. Crummy two-bit temps can be characterised in the first place by the fact that they were hired after proper employment contracts went to hell. As is always the case when things go to hell, this was done with dire consequences for those who came afterwards, and the utmost delicacy for those who came before, in this case or rather, the buddhas. Regardless of their employment sector, these temps' union representatives, when they exist, have practically zero influence and act a bit like kamikazes. Another characteristic of crummy two-bit temps is their chronological age, on average well below that of the buddhas. They make up for this with a pretty poor appearance because they barely have enough money to buy themselves designer clothes (let alone to go on summer holidays or skiing), and because twelve hours a day of actual work are much more damaging to your health than eight hours of simply being present in the office. If a buddha crosses paths with a crummy two-bit temp in the corridor and deigns to look at him, he can relish the fact that, although the crummy two-bit temp may be twenty years his junior, the latter is less tanned, has bags under his eyes so heavy they're literally weighing them down, and has many more gray hairs that he hasn't had time to dye.

According to the most recent figures, the life of a crummy two-bit temp is worth slightly less than that of a wood-louse. If they get sick more than once or twice a year, their contracts are not renewed. If you should happen to tell them at midnight that they have to re-do everything they did that day and they make a face, their contracts are not renewed. If they don't stir the coffee properly, their contracts are not renewed. If the crummy two-bit temp happens to be a secretary and wears trousers rather than a skirt, her contract is not renewed. If they don't smile all the time (in spite of how pathetic it is to smile with bags like that under your eyes) their contracts are not renewed. If they dare to ask what a long weekend is, their contracts are not renewed. There is a catalogue which sets out two hundred and fifty thousand other reasons why a crummy two-bit temp's contract is not open to renewal. They stopped listing further reasons not because there aren't any more, but because they're unnecessary. There is not a single crummy two-bit temp who couldn't be fired three thousand or so times a day on the basis of the reasons already contained in the catalogue.

It might seem that no situation can be worse than that of the crummy two-bit temps. There aren't enough of them and they have to do all the work while the buddhas gleefully cross their way through their betting slips. They aren't well paid, because if they were, how else could their employers afford to pay the buddhas' amazing pensions? They don't have any kind of perks because if they were to have them, the buddhas wouldn't be able to benefit from the generous private medical insurance that allows them to recover so miraculously and completely from their multiple ailments. Furthermore, when they get to a ripe old age (I mean the few who last that long) every cent of their social security contributions will have been spent on guaranteeing the long lives of the buddhas; the only thing they'll get is a kick in the ass.

However, there are those who inspire even more pity. These are the remaining fifth of the seventy per cent of workers who never knew a decent employment contract: the cocksuckers (me, for example). You can find them in what are known as "front-line" professional jobs (not front-line hierarchically speaking, but more like front line as in beachfront, or rather, the landing beach), in commercial banks, stockbrokers, multinational corporations of every description, even, sometimes, in the same companies where the buddhas happily convalesce. The cocksuckers are not crummy two-bit temps: they earn good salaries, in fact, higher than the buddhas themselves. With this alibi, union activity among them is partly inconceivable and partly a show of poor taste. Cocksuckers are young, well-dressed, and they try to be well groomed all the time, which they achieve by various means, some more insane than others. They're allowed to take a long weekend once in a while, they go skiing and on summer holidays they travel abroad. Throughout the rest of the year, they do miserable penance for their sins.

According to the latest figures, the life of a cocksucker is worth slightly less than that of a woodlouse that's had all its little legs torn off. To start with, they work even longer hours than the crummy two-bit temps do. They can't get sick because there's always something urgent they have to do. As a result of this they develop addictions to every kind of medication available in order to stay on their feet come rain or shine. While they soldier on in spite of a fever or choke back the vomit, they may well find themselves having to sign off one of the buddhas who wants to go home to recover more readily from a slight headache. Although officially they are all heads of something, they know how to use the computer, the photocopier, the fax machine and the binding machine, because by the time they've finished their tasks, even the crummy two-bit temps have already gone home (by then, the buddhas who still have children at school have helped them with their homework and put them to bed and are enjoying a whisky in front of the TV). If this wasn't enough, any mistake the cocksuckers make is liable to be punished with violent personal humiliation to which they have no possibility of responding.

Some cocksuckers think this is better than being thrown out on the street, an extreme situation to which they are not subjected as often as the crummy two-bit temps, so they smile while their superiors spit in their faces, thankful for the fact that they are cocksuckers and not crummy two-bit temps. Anyone with half a brain might realize that at least the crummy two-bit temp can look himself in the eye in the mirror. And although they will both die without retirement pension, crummy two-bit temps can foster the hope that their children love them and will take care of them if the worst should happen. But the cocksucker is not only undeserving of his children's respect, but he can't even nurse the hope that they recognize the guy who sometimes showed up at home on weekends and public holidays (but not all of them).

It's hard to explain how so many nice, or good guys and even some relatively worthy individuals, end up weighed down by the curse of being a cocksucker for years and years. Some allow themselves to be blinded by greed or by a meaningless title on a business card. There is always someone who thinks that being a coordinator or earning eighty grand a year places another person who is a mere deputy-coordinator or earns only seventy-nine grand a year a level below them in the food chain. These numbskulls constitute a significant proportion of the population of cocksuckers swarming around the world, and the worrying thing about the world we live in is that there is such an enormous stock of numbskulls that, if necessary, it could more than fill the demand for cocksuckers.

However, a portion of those cocksuckers don't love money (or having thicker business cards than other's) above all else. Those are the cocksuckers whose cocksucking career choice is most surprising, and who are perhaps the most to blame for and the most deserving of their wretched luck, because if they had only decided to get themselves a pair of balls, they could have spared themselves from being so insignificant. However surprising it may seem, these guys are where they are out of vanity. They leapt into the lions' den without considering their actions, or they did so reluctantly, or thinking that they would never want or allow themselves to be swept along by the filthy mainstream. Then they were led into temptation: let's see if you're capable of this and that. They knew they were capable of this and that, and they did it to prove it so that nobody would question their ability ever again. Then one thing led to another, and after that something else, and they were also able to do that too and they proved it once more ... And so on and so on.

When they finally stopped and looked back, they realized they had done a whole heap of things of which they were capable and none of which, however difficult they were, were worth a toss. On the contrary, there was another heap of things that were worth a bit more than a couple of tosses, and which they would have been capable of doing then as well, but after wasting so much time with things that weren't worth a toss, they had become incapable of doing anything else. And the most shameful thing is that instead of taking their car and driving peacefully off a cliff, most of them find consolation by forgetting all about it and continuing to apply themselves diligently to things that aren't worth a toss. They even laugh when they receive pats on the back, desperate for approval, like a poodle being rewarded with a stale biscuit for performing a cute trick.

And this is where the aforementioned pair of balls I was talking about earlier is greatly missed. We're all vain, and everyone likes to be praised for every little thing we do. But it takes a pair of balls to say to the lion tamer asking you to jump through a ring of fire that his fucking mother can do the jumping and he'd better start cracking his whip. The first time you leap through a burning ring of fire you leave your balls hanging there and you can never get them back. For anyone who doesn't already know it, balls are highly flammable.

There was a time when I resisted becoming a cocksucker. I never worshipped money, nor business cards, and

I refused to base my pride on other people admiring my ability to turn somersaults. Those were the days when I had a pair of balls. Then it occurred to me that it's not good for man to live alone, and I asked myself whether it was right to stay on the margins of what the rest of the world, or at least all those who could, were doing. And I felt as capable as anyone else. I gave myself permission to jump through that fucking flaming ring so as not to end up in the gutter and without benefits. I accepted it as a temporary solution until the outlook brightened and I could get my act together. Ten years have passed, give or take. Now I am a cocksucker and I'm more alone than ever.

When I think about these things I always remember Friedrich Nietzsche. I had a religious studies teacher who always took great delight whenever he managed to mention that this atheist had died mad. I was never a fan of good old Friedrich, except when he got his hammer out, but it doesn't seem fair to me that the prize for advocating pride in being a man is having your brains turn to mush and a hundred years later an anthropoid in a dog collar laughs himself silly at your expense in front of a handful of doomed brats.

I might not yet have mentioned that it was summer. This fact is relevant for various other reasons that will become clear, but also because during the summer, banking working hours are shorter and employees leave at noon. Although we cocksuckers almost never take advantage of this perk, it is more or less tolerated that three or four days each summer, on a whim, one can leave the office at the same time as the others, step outside and discover that there is a whole world out there. A world full of parks, birds, children with their mothers and heaps of babes flaunting their navels or wearing skin-tight T-shirts.

So that was exactly what I did the following Thursday: I took the afternoon off, not to go and stare at belly-buttons, but to pursue my strategy of stalking Sonsoles and bringing about her moral downfall. To be more specific, I was interested in carrying out a personal stakeout that would enlighten me as to her habits. This would lead to a series of disconcerting actions that would in turn prompt my chosen victim's fall into disrepute. I would combine slander with several traps until that slut would regret ever meeting me. Now, as I'm writing this, I realize I can barely remember exactly what dirty tricks I had in store for her.

The fact is it doesn't matter a jot. Because that afternoon something happened that screwed everything up and all my best laid plans went to hell. Until that afternoon I had been messing around with Sonsoles in the same way I might have grabbed a handful of silkworms and roasted them in a teaspoon over a Bunsen burner to while away the time. I don't know if I've managed to explain myself. Nothing about what I was doing was essential or particularly appealed to me. And if I'd continued being a spineless motherfucker, probably nothing irreversible would have happened. But that afternoon, betraying all my principles and ignoring the overwhelming teachings of a life of disappointment and lesson-learning, I committed the insane act of allowing myself to fall passionately in love with another human being.

When I was eighteen I wrote a lucid essay entitled "In Praise of Impotence, Cowardice and Other Disqualifications from Transforming Reality", which led to my expulsion from a Maoist literary circle I'd joined without realizing it. Now I have a lot of time on my hands and I've been able to re-read those pages. On one of them is forcefully stated:

In a universe of merciless symmetry, the species seeks the annihilation of the individual to improve his own lot, and the individual can only avoid his misfortune by disregarding the possible fate of the species. Anyone who deigns to pay attention to his fellow human beings, beyond the strictly necessary one to avoid colliding with them, is undoubtedly on the right path to self-destruction.

And the best way to avert this danger is the absence of courage, at times supplemented by pure incompetence. In order to bless the actions of martyrs and condemn those of traitors or the weak, the gregarious spirit has created such a bizarre concept as honour. But reason draws a different conclusion, preferring to absolve anyone acting out of astuteness or necessity to celebrating a show-off's mindless exploits.

Thales of Miletus (or was it Emmanuel from Königsberg-Kaliningrad?) used to say that there is no worse wisdom than premature learning, since this leads to the most terrible ignorance later on. Much to my chagrin, I found out the truth of this ingenious aphorism through my own experience. And I hope that up in the Olympus Zeus is giving the author exactly what he deserves for being right until his ass drops off.

Now I could give you the fact, or facts, in whatever order they come out, but for a bit more variety and a bit less work, I'm going to copy a document. This has two advantages: immediacy, since it was written on the night following the events to which it refers; and intensity, since I was still idiotically moved when I wrote it.

The document reads as follows:

And now, the question: What have I done to waste my life like this? How, of all the possible lives I could have lived, have I ended up living a life made up of nothing but shit and tunnels that don't lead anywhere? A few hours ago I was sitting on a bench in the Retiro park rediscovering these two unanswered questions (or just one, who cares). If I've been carrying them around with me for years without being the least bit upset by them, it can only be because I've been carefully mulling over them like a pious old woman fingering her rosary, without knowing why. Today I've decided to face them head-on. And they've caused me such disgust and sadness that I don't know how I've managed not to dash my brains out against the floor of the inner courtyard for the edification of all the retards who live in my apartment building.

Well, yes, I do know why I haven't done it. Although it pains me to admit it, that is the reason why I have switched on the computer and started to write this confession. The sudden outburst that has led me to face the two damned unanswered questions is also what has kept my skull in one piece.

At the start, nobody would have said that something was going to happen. I'd spent a couple of hours waiting in my car parked opposite the house where the smart-ass slut lives and my mind was already churning up ideas. At exactly six o'clock, the garage's automatic door opens, and Sonsoles' convertible emerges, with her at the wheel. Just as she was a couple of days ago, looking down on everything and everyone, barricaded behind those enormous sunglasses that make her look like a cross between a weasel and an astronaut. I pull out without much enthusiasm and take up position in her wake. My cousin's car, which I've borrowed while they perform plastic surgery on mine, is somewhat short on horse power and I have to put my foot down. Sonsoles drives like a taxi driver, that is, surviving half on her luck, half on the careful driving skills of other drivers and at times demonstrating a mastery at the wheel she could stuff up whatever part of her anatomy she finds most convenient. In order not to lose her, I have to play some dirty tricks on a few innocent drivers, which pisses me off and makes me want to dump her under a UVA lamp and leave her there slowly roasting for ten or twelve days.

Fortunately, the journey is short. Sonsoles leaves her car double parked, while she walks to the entrance of a posh girls' school. A single mother? Inconceivable, given the availability of both abortion and the sacrament of penitence at the same time.

I position myself where I can see the school entrance but am least in the way and I wait. Ten minutes go by. Girls in blue and white uniforms start to come out, dozens of Sonsoles in the bud, dragging out their "s" below their incisors. It is a sight that alternately turns my stomach and awakens morbid desires in me. At last Sonsoles appears, accompanied by a girl or young lady of around fifteen years of age. My heart stops as if they'd pulled the plug on me. Then it happens.

The girl is the most extraordinary thing my sinful eyes have ever seen in all their cocksucking existence. If Sonsoles is her mother, I accept the divine plan that has placed Sonsoles on this planet, however inappropriate this celestial act may have seemed to me up until this moment. If she isn't, the act of going to collect this girl provisionally lends a precious usefulness to her miserable existence. My heart starts beating again, at top speed. It has been centuries since something similar has happened to me and with some effort I order my thoughts, but instinct immediately compensates for lack of habit. Slowly it dawns on me that I've just fallen into a trap. They get into the car and I pull out after them, without resistance, without plans, without a hope.

From that moment on Sonsoles, who until then I have persecuted, becomes no more than a fuzzy blob escorting this disturbing adolescent goddess. The girl fills everything with her presence. I can even see her if I close my eyes: she is tall, her body, not yet in full bloom, long hair flowing in the wind like those stunning nymphs that rascal Botticelli used to paint, and a blue gaze so immense that distance doesn't matter. I vaguely remember that I've never been attracted to blondes, but she isn't a woman, and the effect she has on me is more than mere physical attraction. As everyone knows, the garbage cans of the spirit are overflowing with mere physical attractions.

The rest is too fleeting. I follow them as far as Calle Serrano, where they enter a store where the price of all the clothes is rounded up in multiples of ten thousand pesetas. Of course I would have liked to follow them into the changing rooms, by which I mean the girl's changing room, but my mere presence in the shop would have been too suspicious. When they get back in the convertible, freeing a guy whose car has been blocked in by Sonsoles' for a quarter of an hour, the girl is carrying a couple of bags and Sonsoles has about six. They don't stow them in the trunk because it looks much better when you carelessly throw them on the back seat, over the convertible's bodywork. Also because the trunk is a sight to behold as a result of the bash I gave it the other day. They climb in and I tail them again. When we stop at a traffic light, the girl sweeps her hair to one side and starts looking at one of the cops who go around showing off on their motorbikes and dismounting from time to time to direct the traffic at a crossroads. The local police cowboy is struck down on the spot, his whistle dangling from his lips, upright only thanks to his biker boots, mortally naked faced with his own insignificance. Five minutes later, the garage door of Sonsoles' building opens again, and the convertible is swallowed up by the subterranean darkness. End of the apparition.

Let's say it is quarter past seven. Day is not over and the sun is still up in the sky, but nothing makes sense anymore. There I am, sitting in a borrowed car, watching with my soul smashed to smithereens as the door closes with a clang that plunges me into deepest night. Disappointment and depressing thoughts don't usually bother me, because my garden is overrun with all their weeds and I've even learned to sculpt them into hedges. But this bitterness has disarmed me and overpowered me in a way I no longer remembered possible. I think I've experienced this before. Perhaps the time when I went to a raffle with other children and one of them won the bicycle I yearned so much for and I got a stupid tank that fired rubber suckers instead of bullets. Perhaps when we were playing forfeits and Paloma, who had skin like porcelain, was condemned to kiss me and I felt the combination of her soft cheek and her repulsion and afterwards I saw her go away forever. Perhaps when my mother died on my nineteenth birthday and I suddenly turned a hundred years old.

I look for a parking place and head towards the Retiro. I go through the gate and hurriedly follow a path that leads me to a secluded spot in the park. I sit on a bench and stare at the trees. It is hot, I feel uncomfortable. I dodge the two questions for a while, but in the end I ask myself: What have I done to waste my life like this? How, of all the possible lives I could have lived, have I ended up living a life made up of nothing but shit and tunnels that don't lead anywhere?

In general terms, I don't give a damn about all the things I can't do or have: that's the advantage of thinking that everything you see is a piece of shit or is well on the way to becoming it. What is bad is when you see something that obviously isn't a piece of shit, and at the same time you realize it's beyond your reach. That is the moment of humiliation, and nobody likes to be humiliated. A poor devil, in other words me, can get through life for a long while by playing the cynic, although he doesn't stop being a poor devil. Until you are humiliated. Then you have to run and hide where nobody will find you and burst into tears, with snot and all the works. You rediscover in yourself the fragile, disappointed child on which every adult's personality is built, and at the same time you recover the longing to fulfil your dreams, and the impossibility of doing so. It doesn't matter how much you run or how tall you are: this feeling shatters you. There are very brave and clever people out there, but it's too complicated to be a tough guy when you're sniffling away.

This afternoon I stayed there under the trees until it got really dark and I began to run the risk that some evil character might come and slash my guts open and take my credit cards (or rather the other way round, because if they slash you open first, they'll have a helluva time finding out your pin number). Then I got the car and drove slowly under the city lights. Now here I sit, seeking solace from this stupid machine, but the machine only does what I tell it to, and can only reflect my astonishment back at me in fluorescent lines.

I must explain why I accept my fate, which is the most shameful thing of all. I squeeze my eyelids shut and I see her, moving, smiling, her amazing blue eyes darting here and there. And I think: Is it remotely possible for me to get her? I ought to know that the answer is no, or worse, that even if this did come to pass, it would all turn into dust, into shit, into nothing. I ought to accept that's how it is and draw the consequences. But if I'm writing, and not lying on the floor of the inner courtyard with my head smashed to bits, it's because I haven't accepted it. When I was still able to believe it, this restlessness meant being alive. Now it is something that offends whoever has decreed I must die. May my punishment, when it comes, not be too painful.

And so, with this confession of guilt and even malice aforethought, I forgot the comfortable, petty stalking of Sonsoles and hastened my doom. To all those who, like me, find the ridiculous lyricism of the last few pages I've just written rather odd, all I can say in my defense is that at that time I was suffering a chemically induced melancholia which meant I was unquestionably quite vulnerable. After several years of doubt, I had ended up losing faith in psychiatrists and benzodiazepines. I don't know if that can justify things, but perhaps it helps to explain it better. In those circumstances, and after having spent a couple of days toying with the gloomy idea of having some fun with Sonsoles, that young girl was too strong a temptation. I admit it's possible that I'm nothing more than a pervert. But I suspect that, in my position, even Emmanuel from Königsberg Kalininigrad himself would have said to hell with the categorical imperative and stopped telling his neighbors where to get off, in order to lie on his bed and dream of the abject delights of paedophilia.

Of all the striking photographs in the world, there is one that inspires awe regardless of ideology or prejudice: the one of the four Russian grand duchesses, the daughters of Nicholas II who were put to the sword (of whatever sort) by the Bolsheviks in Yekaterinburg after the Revolution. It doesn't matter whether you're atheist or orthodox, reactionary communist or an econotechnoliberal, a supporter of the monarchy or someone who believes that every last drop of blue blood should be poured down the drain as soon as possible. Those four perfect faces, those four proud and angelic children, forever united by their tragic destiny, leave an indelible impact on whatever small piece of heart we may have left.

I keep their photograph on my desk (well, let's call it that) here as in all the other places I've lived over the past five years since I discovered it. I've looked at it so often I know it by heart. It's difficult to choose one from among the four girls. They all have that elusive Slav beauty, partly divine, partly wild. The same beauty that the best ice-skaters and gymnasts possess (apart from the American ones, so vulgar with their orthodontic braces), a beauty that has led me to become addicted to their competitions. However, if I had to choose my favourite, for example if someone were to threaten me with doing something as cruel as taking a pair of scissors to the photograph, I would beg him to spare the Grand Duchess Olga.

Of the four, she is the eldest and perhaps the haughtiest. She stares right at the camera, fully aware of her boundless charm, like a professional. The others hold their heads erect, but she tilts hers to the side, with calculated languor. At her young age she is already imbued with her semi-divine status and knows that the photographer is a lackey, little more than a muzhik. The Grand Duchess floats in a dress that is worth and costs (not that she's paying) more than everything the photographer owns. She has no reason to fear him, and she proclaims this through her childish insolence, tinged with a precocious hint of the femme fatale.

I've repeatedly asked myself what that girl, that budding young woman, felt when she saw the first rifletouting muzhik burst into her chambers to trample on the cloud of tulle in which she had lived until that moment. When she had to suffer in silence as her beautiful flesh paid for all the muzhik blood spilled by the despots adorning her family tree. I've never read, although maybe it's been written down somewhere, exactly what they did to the grand duchesses before dispatching them to the common grave so that nobody could plant a possible Czar of all the Russias in their bellies. Of course I've imagined it, naturally, and not always in a virtuous way. At the age the Grand Duchess Olga was when she was forever cut off from the line of succession, she must have been a creature eminently capable of arousing impure thoughts and acts, and it's debatable whether an inflamed Bolshevik would have turned his nose up or repressed his manhood. The Russians' propensity for lust and torturing their neighbors is as notorious as their propensity to wail away to a background of balalaikas. Therefore, assuming a probable situation (whether it happened or not is neither here nor there), I have also often asked myself what the Grand Duchess felt when the first muzhik ripped off his cartridge belt and howled with pleasure. The feelings an ordinary woman would experience are well-known, but not those of a Grand Duchess, accustomed to thinking of muzhiks as being on the same level as dogs, or lower, depending on the dog.

I can't deny that on imagining this horrible scene I find myself taking sides with the Grand Duchess against the Bolshevik. In the first place, I'm sure the Grand Duchess washed herself more often, and she spoke French. When you're walking down a deserted street at night (life is a dark and deserted street at night), and you turn a corner, you would rather come across a sweet-smelling young lady who speaks French than a muzhik crawling with lice. Secondly, although the idea is a bit too despicable for people to easily admit, any male who finds himself attracted by a female feels a physiological hatred towards the guy who gets to have her, regularly or as a one-off.

So, having made clear my devoted commitment to the Grand Duchess, it is nevertheless undeniable that I have never been able to put myself in her shoes, whereas I have tried the Bolshevik's on for size. There's a moment in particular when the Bolshevik's fate sends a shiver down my spine. Not when he finds her, not even when he strips her and discovers her divine treasure (maybe the brute didn't even bother to strip her). Nor, of course, when he defiles her, taking her like any other woman and dispossessing her of her Grand Duchy. No, the moment when the Bolshevik discovers his elusive mission here on Earth occurs after the Grand Duchess has been assassinated and buried, when he remembers her for the first time.

Until then, he has been able to seek refuge in the mob he belongs to. But at that moment he is on his own. Filtered through memory for the first time, his feelings about the Grand Duchess are something that concern only him. And the damsel's martyrdom and death don't have the same meaning for him as for the others. The rest of them barely are aware of anything except for the black pleasure of revenge. He on the other hand, falling into an ambush of destiny, suffers a loss. The Cause demanded that she be executed, and he believed in the Cause. How many muzhiks died during the reign of Nicholas II? Until this moment, the answers to simple questions like that protected him. But now no more. He wishes the little girl hadn't disappeared, and the Cause is responsible for his devastation. The Cause and himself.

What a tender moment, when the Bolshevik turns against himself and the Revolution to admit his already necessarily despairing love for the Grand Duchess. When he forgets that the sweet memory he surrenders to was refined over the centuries thanks to the blood and sweat of his own ancestors. There is no more interesting believer than the one who changes faith. An unswerving patriot, an unrelenting revolutionary, a chaste monk, prompt yawns as easily as approving epitaphs. The world progresses thanks to renegades.

I've always thought that the paradise where the heroes go, Valhalla or whatever it's called, must be a gloomy place where trumpets blow, banners fly in the air, and athletic hetaerae perform laborious sexual gymnastics with the champions. On the other hand, the den where felons wallow must be a place worthy of fantasy: it must be swarming with the most complex women, with whom it's possible to hold substantial conversations. Nor is it a question, in my view, of spending all day mating like monkeys, to obtain the tedious reward that for an alarming number of cultures is the only thing that brainless idiots who die for a sublime idea seem to want.

Like everyone else, I've got my revolutionary side, and I find it somewhat trying to praise the genocides encouraged or tolerated by the Czars as part of their empire-building whims. It's worth pointing this out so that what I'm about to state is not misunderstood: of everything that happened in the Russian Revolution, nothing affects me more than the faint-heartedness of this Bolshevik, overwhelmed by his filthy passion for the tyrant's daughter. Perhaps such a Bolshevik never existed, and it's undeniable that the revolution was the epic culmination of a powerful belief. Even so, I stand by what I've said. Beliefs invariably follow a natural course, from their revolt against another wicked belief to their transformation into the new wickedness that will later have to be destroyed. Pain and beauty, on the other hand, are irrefutable because they cannot be measured against any belief, nor do they require any belief to be at their service. No man is worth what he believes in, but instead what he has desired and what he has been given to suffer. Any son of a bitch or dimwit can believe whatever they like. The chosen ones are chosen for ecstasy or misfortune. The best, for both.

I contemplate the distant image of Olga with her sisters, all destined for torture (at least we can be sure of the moral torture) and execution. Who would have thought, when everything I've written was nothing more than nonsense to while away Sunday afternoons, that I would find myself one day experiencing the Bolshevik's guilty faint-heartedness?

The fact is, the body knows what's best for it, and sometimes so does the brain bubbling away up top, so that the next morning, I no longer remembered having harboured sinister thoughts regarding myself and that highly disconcerting young girl. I might go so far as to say I was in a peculiarly good mood. There was a time when my ability to switch from despair to light-heartedness with the same ease as swapping one tie for another bothered me, but since I discovered that being cyclothymic protects against other more tiring and unpleasant mental illnesses, I have happily welcomed my mood swings.

While I made coffee I decided I was sick and, putting on my most pitiful voice, I called the office to let them know. I would have time later to come up with something serious enough to justify my abandoning ship for the day. I took off my tie, but while I was taking off my going-to-the-bank shirt to exchange it for my lucky one (which has an indelible mark on the front, the result of a red-headed bombshell puking on me during a rather mysterious work dinner), it occurred to me it might be of some use dressing up a bit. I therefore reassembled my normal image as a respectable guy, in the usual sense of the term. By this I mean I looked more like the kind of bastards who, if they want to screw you over, pay someone else to do it, rather than the kind of bastards who screw you over because someone's paid them to do it (decent people don't have a definite appearance; you recognize them after a while because they haven't screwed you over). I'm ashamed to admit it, but it's also possible that I splashed on a bit more Paco Rabanne or Armani, which is what jerks like me do once we get past thirty, to disguise the stench of decay.

When I left home I didn't have a concrete strategy, but I already knew I was going to approach the girl and push my luck. I brushed aside everything that told me I should leave her alone and everything that had depressed me the previous afternoon. I was nothing but a filthy, unscrupulous pig, and that little darling was but a promise of sordid delights. That being the case, things were bound to happen.

I got to the school after registration, when the girls were already all in class.

For a while I indulged in some hare-brained ideas: passing myself off as an inspector from the Ministry of Education, there to give the owners of that select teaching establishment a headache; posing as an exec from an advertising agency looking for cute little girls to advertise mini tampons; going in wearing dark glasses and suggesting to a member of staff that human trafficking could provide a healthy supplement to their meagre wages. But when it came down to it I couldn't be bothered, so I thought it better to wait until the break. The wall around the playground was low and by taking up position by the railings I might be able to see something.

Break began at eleven. The girls came out in year groups and arranged themselves around a skipping rope here, a hopscotch over there, a mysterious joint glowing in one of the girl's hands somewhere else. I was a bit surprised that such well-brought up young ladies, who had so many reasons (and genuine ones at that, not the ones they use to convince poor devils to abstain) to say no to drugs, should prove to be such unashamed hash addicts. It was by pure chance that I was stationed at the point furthest from the school building and that this little group had come to almost fifty feet of me the better to conduct their clandestine activities. I pretended I hadn't seen what they were up to, but my presence didn't put them off. The girl rolling the joint glanced at me, then carried on what she was doing.

At first there were five of them, but gradually another three drifted over from the middle of the playground. One of the trio was my girl. All of them were about fourteen or fifteen years old, and their bodies were a chaotic mixture of woman and girlish features, but she stood out from the rest. She was the tallest, the most attractive, the only one without a single pimple on her face and the juiciest by far. She had barely joined the group when the girl busy rolling the joint snapped at her, "Are you going to have a drag today, Rosana, or does the idea of sucking on something we've all sucked on put you off?"

"You're such a dyke, Izaskun," trilled Rosana in a bored tone.

"And you so fussy, Miss fucking little princess."

"I'm not fussy, it's just that I've got my own," replied Rosana, producing a pack of Marlboros and a pink lighter from the waistband of her skirt. She lit a cigarette and began to smoke, her arms crossed, her hips, as yet not rounded like a woman's, pushed forward.

"You're missing out. There's no comparison," said Izaskun, "but perhaps if you smoke a joint you won't be top of the class and that senile Doña Lourdes will stop going on about how you're going to be a doctor or a government minister."

"Drop it, Izaskun, you're always bugging her," one of the others cut in.

"I'm not going to be anything like that," Rosana defended herself, "but I'm not going to end up like you, advertising yourself in the papers to get money to buy coke."

"Have you tried coke, Izaskun?" asked the one who seemed the stupidest member of the clique.

"Once," bragged Izaskun, shooting Rosana a resentful look. "My cousin gave me some to try when we did it."

"The only thing you've done is pee on your bed while dreaming about it," Rosana mocked her. Some of the others laughed.

"What about you?" asked the dimwit, eager for sordid details of whatever vice someone else might have been engaging in.

"As if I'd tell you."

"Of course she has, Nuria," Izaskun laughed, "With Ken, Barbie's boyfriend. She put his head right up there. His dick's tiny, even by her standards."

Now it was the girls who had been with Izaskun before Rosana and her friends arrived who burst out laughing. Rosana kept quiet, exhaling smoke with her top lip arched as if she were about to smile. Then she turned and walked off with her two friends.

As soon as the girls went back inside I rushed to find a phone booth. I dialled Sonsoles' number and was greeted by the hoarse voice of Lucía, the maid:

"Hello?"

"Good morning, I'm calling from Rosana's school, is that her mother?"

"No."

"In that case, with whom am I speaking?"

"I'm the maid."

"Ah. Is the lady of the house there?"

"Yes, one moment."

After about thirty seconds, the unmistakable sound of Sonsoles' mother came down the line. "What can I do for you?"

"Good morning madam, I'm calling from your daughter's school. We'd like to arrange a meeting between you and her tutor."

"Has something happened?"

"No, quite the opposite, please don't worry. We're arranging meetings for all the girls at the moment. It's part of their career guidance programme. They're reaching an age where they ought to start thinking about the future. Rosana is a very good student."

"Yes, she is."

"And a very reliable girl."

"She's never given us any trouble at all," said the mother of Sonsoles and Rosana, her pride once again evident in her voice.

"When would suit you?"

"Please, I'll leave it to you to decide."

Now I had the information I was after (Sonsoles *was not* the girl's mother), I got rid of the woman as quickly as I could, inviting her to a meeting the following Monday that nobody would attend and whose only consequence would be that she would be furious with the school to which Don Armando paid such high fees. Misfortune is sometimes the result of stupid lapses in foresight.

The girls were let out at half past twelve and Rosana and a few friends caught a bus. I got back in the car and followed it to Sonsoles' house. Rosana got off with another blonde girl, although her shade of blond was more washed out. I heard them arrange to meet a quarter of an hour later and parked nearby.

Fifteen minutes later, the two girls were reunited and set off towards the Retiro park. Once inside, they went in search of an ice cream stand and bought a couple of cones. They walked as far as the pond and followed the path around the northern side. They sat on a bench near the statue of Ramón y Cajal to finish their ice creams. While they were sitting there, the other girl looked at Rosana and Rosana looked straight ahead. Rosana seemed serious and was doing the talking. The other girl wasn't saying much, only giggled every so often. I was on the far side of the path, so I couldn't hear them over the noise other people made. After a few minutes they were joined by another girl. She'd got off the bus one stop before them.

Half an hour later, the one who had come with Rosana looked at her watch and said something to her. Sonsoles' sister shook her head. After wavering for a few moments, the one with the watch got up and left. Rosana stayed with the other girl for another ten minutes, smoking and talking in a low voice. After that they said goodbye and went their separate ways. Rosana set off slowly down the path, looking at the trees and the passers-by. If I had been her age, or if things had been different, I would've followed her home discreetly and then gone back to my house to write her some poetry. But things were what they were: I was thirty-three and had little or no desire to write any poems, so I asked myself why I was putting it off. That moment was as good as any. I started to follow her and three or four metres before I caught up with her I called out, "Rosana."

She stopped and turned round very slowly. She looked more wary than astonished.

"How do you know my name?"

"Don't be afraid," I said, lifting my hands in a sign of peace.

"I'm not afraid. Who are you?"

"I'm Javier, and I'm a friend."

"A friend of whom?" The pupils of her blue eyes were so small they'd almost disappeared.

"Okay. I'm a policeman. But don't tell anyone."

"I've done nothing wrong," she said firmly, and set off again, but in a leisurely way, as if aware that I would walk alongside her. I caught up with her.

"I know. I want to talk to you about your friend Izaskun."

"You must have made a mistake. I don't have any friends by that name."

"There aren't so many Rosanas around that I'd make a mistake."

"Whatever. None of my friends are called Izaskun."

I smiled and tried to catch her eye, but it was impossible unless she was the one catching yours.

"It's no good trying to trick me. I know she's in your class and I've seen you with her at school. You were together in the playground today."

"That doesn't mean we're friends," she pointed out, flicking her hair back with her right hand, which was the one nearest me. Normally the best way of telling a girl isn't a woman yet is by looking at her hands: girls' hands tend to have stubby fingers and chewed nails. Rosana's nails were short, although she didn't bite them, but there was nothing stubby about her fingers. On the contrary, she separated them and moved them like a pro, demonstrating a sophistication that many women never acquire, aware that each finger has its own task in life.

"Rosana, you're a good girl," I said, "and you know that Izaskun is in trouble. Wouldn't you like to help her?"

"Help Izaskun? I'd be glad if you put her in prison. She's a complete idiot and deserves it."

"We won't be putting any girls in prison. It's not exactly little girls we're after."

"Well, what can I do?"

"Tell me who sells her drugs. That's all."

"Borja. He's her pusher."

"Borja who?"

"I don't know. He goes to the boys' school next to ours, the one run by priests."

Rosana had changed direction. She came to a halt under one of the trees by the side of the path to make her accusation in greater comfort. I stood facing her.

"Is there no way you can give me his last name? There could be five hundred Borjas in that school."

Rosana raised her eyes and looked me up and down for a moment. Then she said, "This Borja is unmistakable, he's been repeating eighth grade for three or four years and they're always trying to kick him out. They'd have done it already, except his dad's president of the Alumni Association."

"Do you know anything else about him?"

"Yes. He's always trying to hook up with me," she boasted, twisting one of her curls around her index finger, "but since I don't pay him any attention he goes out with Izaskun instead. Izaskun has got a strong stomach."

"And that's everything you know?"

"And that's everything I know, cop," she snapped at me.

"Wow, you watch lots of movies, don't you?"

"Sometimes. I also saw you earlier, by the school railings. I thought you were one of those guys who like to spy on the girls skipping in case they show their underwear."

"Well, I suppose there are quite a few guys like that."

"A few. But they never wear such nice ties as yours. I noticed it before. I didn't think cops earned much."

"I work overtime. Do you like coming to the park?"

Rosana frowned. "What's that got to do with your investigation?"

"Nothing. I've finished questioning you. It's to learn more about you. I've taken a liking to you."

Rosana moved away from the tree.

"I don't think you're so bad yourself. But Lucía will have had lunch on the table five minutes ago. My mother gets angry if I'm late. She says Lucía won't take preparing it seriously if I'm late. Have you any idea how difficult it is to find decent help these days?" she asked sarcastically.

"Of course, you're right. I won't keep you. Thanks a lot for everything."

"There's no need to thank me. I think it's great you're going to arrest Borja."

"You mustn't tell anyone. Not even your mother or your best friend."

"You can't tell my mother anything. Poor thing. Goodbye."

"See you later," I replied, spell-bound.

Rosana moved away down the path, her impeccable mane of blonde hair waving in the wind as she moved through the crowd. At one point she pushed her hair to one side and took advantage of the opportunity to turn her head and check whether I was watching her. I could make out the look of pleasure on her face in spite of the distance between us. It was ten past two and it was starting to get too hot to be wearing a suit, but it wasn't too bad standing there in the shadow of the trees. I wandered among the elderly, the children and the beautiful girls on skates, their slim thighs wrapped in dazzling multi-coloured leggings. One of the disadvantages of summer is that you can get distracted and imagine there are no ugly women in the world. As I walked I remembered Lewis Carroll and J. M. Barrie, perhaps two of the most brilliant apostles of heterosexual pederasty (although there are some who maintain that Barrie swung both ways, I don't believe so: just think about the nervous shiver Peter Pan feels when he discovers that Wendy has become a mother and compare that with the complete indifference he shows the boys). I also remembered Oscar Wilde, unparalleled apostle of the other kind of pederasty. It ought to give pause for thought that some of the most distinguished members of society figure among those who devote themselves to activities society considers appalling. The Greeks, to whom we Europeans owe the glorious inheritance of doubt that distinguishes us from backward peoples and savages (for example North America, Japan, etc.) were almost all sodomites or child molesters. Of course, it's always been easier to burn at the stake those who do things that make their fellow citizens feel uneasy. Perhaps that is what every self-respecting ruler should do. But what might the irresponsible subject prefer to do?

When I still enjoyed the idea of seeing the world, I took advantage of a summer holiday to go to Paris. There is a cemetery there called Père Lachaise, and that is where Oscar Wilde is buried. His tomb is an unbearably tacky affair funded by an admirer, but behind it there's a shelf loaded with curious objects. They are mementoes left by visitors: stones, dried flowers, metro tickets, locks of hair, letters. Among the latter I discovered one which began: "Dear Oscar, Since you left us, things in England haven't changed much ... " This was followed by the moving confession of the spiritual torments of a closet gay, an impressive filigree of exquisite feelings. After reading it I had a curious thought: Would anyone be the slightest bit moved by a letter left by a straight guy on the tomb of, for argument's sake, one of the honourable members of the jury that condemned Oscar?

That day, and I didn't realize until the end of the afternoon, when I went to Rosana' s school and nobody came out, was a Friday. In June, public schools don't have classes in the afternoon, but in those where the wealthy pay fees (where they stow away their offspring for safe keeping far from their servants' vulgar influence, while they go about their important business) Fridays are the only half day in the whole academic year. It must be because it's increasingly common for the urban warrior to begin his weekend rest period on Friday afternoon.

Fridays always throw me off center. Sometimes I end up going to one of those bars where you find affection-starved divorcés and divorcées. The kind of place where women give you their phone number the moment they tell you their name and always carry condoms in their handbags. For the most part it's boring, but from time to time I've met some very sensitive people who simply feel lost in the midst of a mess that caught them off guard. Society has no pity for those who break down and fall through its cracks. Besides which, they're forty years old and the men realize that their eyes aren't crinkling the way Robert

Mitchum's do and the women that their butts aren't quite as tight as Jane Fonda's.

Other times I feel less philosophical and head to one of those temples that resound with the rubbish that acts as a tom-tom for the spoiled brats who stuff themselves with pills then go out and kill themselves on the motorway crashing into some innocent father on his way home from the night shift. Once there I normally get drunk as quickly as possible while I pass the time watching spoiled little girls dancing, since there's a well-known law of physics that determines that the density of their gray matter is inversely proportional to the length of their legs and the firmness of their tits.

The number of long legged people around these days is incredible, in a country known for its short legged population. The number of blondes and Business Administration graduates is also amazing. They must have put something in the food that's caused a spate of genetic mutations, because we were never like that before. One of my family heirlooms is a picture of a handful of soldiers and NCOs posing with four mules during the Africa campaign taken around 1924. One of them is my grandfather, who had to do his military service there, or rather, to fight in the war, which was what men were forced to do at the time, although nobody claimed to be a conscientious objector (a conscience isn't a basic commodity, just a whim of people with full stomachs). If those dark skinned men in rags could see their great-grandchildren dancing acid under blaring laser lights they'd think they were witnessing the end of the world. And vice versa: on more than one occasion a gum-chewer passing through my apartment to do the only thing you can do with gum-chewers has stopped in front of the photo and asked me why I had all those horrible Turks up on my wall.

But I was in the middle of that Friday afternoon after I had made contact with Rosana and, in front of the gates of her deserted school, I was weighing the pros and cons of a series of unenticing alternatives for filling the rest of the day. Since it was still a few hours until nightfall, I decided to head over to the López-Díaz apartment and sit outside for a couple of hours in the car, waiting for something to happen. Perhaps Rosana might come out. Or Sonsoles would, and catch me exhausted from the long wait.

I'd say I spent almost two and a half hours there, posted opposite the entrance. When the door opened and Rosana came out, the light was starting to fade and I was beginning to doze off. She'd replaced her school uniform with a pair of jeans that showed off all her curves and a vest top that didn't quite cover her midriff. As she'd done in the morning, she walked unhurriedly up the street that led from her building to the Retiro park. Even when she'd disappeared from view I still couldn't decide whether or not it was a good idea to follow her. Perhaps it was enough to leave things as they were for the day. But I couldn't resist the temptation to spy on her. If I'd been given the chance, I would have sold my soul for a good picture of her naked shoulders.

Rosana walked up as far as the pond. She wandered amongst the musicians, puppeteers, fortune tellers and trinket sellers. Then she spent ten minutes leaning on the railing, watching the boats. A kid of about her age tried to strike up a conversation and she listened to him silently until he gave up and went away. Then she moved away from the railing and walked down the path that leads to the small square with the statue of the Fallen Angel, which she ignored. She was heading for the rose garden, where she found a seat and made herself comfortable to watch the sunset.

Two powerful sensations grew within me as I watched her. The first one was a most unhealthy envy towards that blessed creature who could devote herself to watching sunsets and didn't have to waste her time for a fistful of filthy money. I remembered that scamp Joseph de Maistre, and how right he was was when he declared that only those with private incomes who find themselves exempt from the squalor of a regular job have time to cultivate the spirit and are therefore able to consider the problems of the Republic with equanimity. The rest of us are resentful sods who can, in the best case scenario, become dangerous criminals (examples of humble men who unfairly attained power: Napoleon, Durruti, Himmler).

The second sensation concerns something I owe, paradoxically, to Dostoevsky. I am one of the few men alive who can say they've read *The Brothers Karamazov* from cover to cover; I undertook such an enormous sacrifice with the sole aim of being able to say from first hand knowledge that old Fyodor Mikhailovich was real hard going. But Dostoevsky is also the author of a short story entitled "White Nights", which I not only liked, but which had a lasting influence on me. It is the story of a woman who goes for solitary walks and in just a few nights the main character falls madly in love with her. Ever since I read it—I reckon I was very impressionable at the time—

women who walk alone have inevitably stolen my heart. Sitting there, watching the sunset at the end of the afternoon, Rosana awoke that irrational fascination in me. If I were a general or a minister, the enemy could drag every last state secret I possessed out of me just by sending a spy who could sit still on a park bench meditating. She wouldn't even have to be beautiful, just as long as she didn't have any visible deformities. Whenever I've told anyone this, they've immediately assumed that I fall in love all the time. Nothing could be further from the truth. Nowadays it's extraordinarily difficult to find women (or men) who meditate. Especially not on a park bench, even if someone were holding a gun to their heads.

Rosana wasn't in any rush. She remained at her post until the sky turned a shade of violet and I started to wonder how her family let her run the risk of being in the Retiro park as night began to fall. It's true that there were still quite a few people around, but the rose garden was starting to empty. When she finally got up and started on her way, I took a moment to do a quick calculation. Before she left the rose garden I ran to a path that she would be forced to take if she headed home. I chose a bench and sat down.

I saw her coming, lost in thought, taking her time. I was hoping that she would spot me, but she walked right past me and I had to attract her attention.

"Rosana."

She stopped walking and turned towards me. It took her a second to recognize me.

"What are you doing here?"

"I come here for a walk every evening," I replied. "What about you?"

"Nothing."

"Why don't you take a seat?" I invited her, bluntly. "It's nice here."

"My mother says I shouldn't talk to strangers. I think that's equally true of the unemployed guys who sell packs of kleenex at traffic lights and policemen who wear fancy ties."

"Do you always do what your mother says?"

Rosana came a couple of steps closer, close enough for me to be filled with an unbearable desire to jump on her and bite her shoulders. As if this wasn't enough to turn me into a drooling beast—and it was—I realized she wasn't wearing a bra. She had a pair of perfect little things, light as birds.

"No," she said.

"Well then."

Rosana looked away.

"Is Javier your real name?"

"Yes."

"I like that name. Are you a real policeman?"

"Yes to that too."

The girl looked at me again. Her pupils were shining.

"Have you arrested Borja yet?" she asked.

"No, not yet. We need to check a few more things."

"I thought you might lie to me. Borja rang me this afternoon. He was sitting at home, calm as could be."

"You're a very smart kid. But if you carry on standing there you'll grow and you won't be a girl anymore. You might even stop being so bright."

She took a step back. The sky was already dark.

"It's very late. I can't stay."

"Lucía already has supper ready," I guessed.

"You're good with names."

"It's how I earn a living."

"Lucía had the afternoon off. It's my mother's turn to cook."

I leant back and tried to resist her spell. It was better not to start anything I wasn't in a position to finish.

"Then you ought to go. I wouldn't want your mother to be angry with you on my account."

"You'll think I'm trying to get away from you," she whined and I couldn't tell whether she was joking or speaking seriously.

"No. I'm going to do something. Tomorrow at eleven I'll come and sit on this bench. If you're here by eleven fifteen we'll talk without you having to run off anywhere. If you're not, I'll get the message and leave and we will never speak to each other again. What do you say?"

Rosana laughed.

"I'm not promising anything. I get up late on Saturdays. If you were still here at noon, I might be here, but I still couldn't promise."

"Eleven fifteen, not a minute later. If you're not here at eleven fifteen then I'll know you don't care. Sweet dreams, sleep tight."

"I'm too old for sweet dreams. I had my first period three years ago."

"Wow."

"And I know what you're after, in case you think I haven't noticed," she announced proudly.

"I don't think you really know. And if you get here after eleven fifteen tomorrow you'll never find out."

"Of course I will. When one of these days you go back to catch a glimpse of the girls' panties when they skip rope at the playground. Then don't pretend you're a policeman."

"I didn't make it up. But you can think whatever you like, Rosana. You're too pretty to have regrets."

"Goodbye."

"See you tomorrow."

She left and when night fell over the park completely I was still sitting on the bench, lost in memories of her shoulders and conjuring unmentionable dreams.

That Friday night I skipped my usual pastimes and stayed home, drowning my sorrows in a bottle of Black Bush I'd bought in some airport somewhere. My body managed to absorb about half of it: I poured the rest ceremoniously down the toilet. My CD player was on at full blast in the background, the final nail in the coffin of any civilized relationship with my neighbors, playing the low notes of that sumptuous melody the world owes to Alison Moyet with the most perfect title anyone has ever come up with: "Winter Kills".

In this day and age, overwhelmed by the media, that either drone on about how we should go and see a film about that pretentious cornball Beethoven, or instead beatify some English-speaking lout who died of an overdose despite the fact that he didn't even know how to hold a guitar properly, people don't dare say what they really think about music. It's tough to admit that what Mahler did and what Mick Jagger does are the same thing, but you realize that you can't say anything against either of them, so most people come to believe they don't have any taste and they'd better keep quiet or repeat whatever the TV or the press tells them.

I am aware that like everyone else I've been gagged in this way, and the few times I've tried to rise up against it, the person I was talking to hurled such a ton of official crap that I was almost left without any arguments. I say almost because I always had at least one, which I used to keep to myself, but I don't mind sharing now: the only worthwhile music is music that moves me, and the kind of music that moves me is the music that I fucking want to be moved by.

During my lost years, many different types of music moved me, partly because I didn't correctly identify what music was and partly because I didn't correctly identify what it meant to be moved. I even thought myself moved by Haydn, which is clearly a slip-up. Having reflected on the matter, I now understand that a man needs to travel light, so I've stuck with the essentials. I've reduced the entirety of musical history to the following list, which is more than enough for my needs: *Upstairs at Eric's* by Yazoo, *The Number of the Beast* by Iron Maiden, and Schubert.

The fact that the list is so short doesn't mean I don't listen to other types of music. As you will remember, this whole ill-fated story began with a smash caused by Judas Priest. What it means is that, except for the music I've just listed, I refrain from *listening*.

I'll start with Schubert. How is it possible that nothing he composed is unnecessary? Perhaps the trick is to barely eke out a living, to be as lonely as a dog and to die at thirty. To give a contrasting example, Bach lived to a ripe old age, had a bunch of kids and stuffed his face (you only need to look at his double chin to see that). With regard to the merits of his music—I'm talking about Schubert here—I'll leave it to other people to sum up the universally accepted reasons you have to reel off in polite society to prevent a shitty know-it-all shutting your mouth for you. That's not what interests me here. I've rescued Schubert and placed him above all others because the first and only time I believed I had fallen in love in a respectable manner, his Trio Op. 100 was playing in the background. It's also because the first time I was more or less serious about throwing myself off the viaduct (this is harking back to when I was an idiot and didn't shit in my pants at the thought of death like I do now), I took a Walkman with *Winterreise* on it (as well as an idiot, I was a sensationalist) and listened to it all the way through to the end (by which point I'd forgotten I'd gone there to commit suicide). But perhaps more than anything else I love Schubert because even today, when the first movement of his Fifth Symphony starts, I am assailed by the astonishing conviction of having been truly happy at some point in my life.

The reasons that come to mind for choosing *The Number of the Beast* are less nostalgic. Although I limited myself to this particular album, I do admit that there's enough on their first two albums (*Iron Maiden* and *Killers*) for them to claim they'd peaked at that early stage. For me, they could have saved themselves the trouble when it comes to all the music that came after that (I do understand though that they had families to feed). It was already a kind of premonition that the final track on the album, *Hallowed Be Thy Name*, was the lament of a death row inmate. There's no denying that none of the other tracks equals the perfection of this last one, those fleeting minutes when heavy metal reaches an absolute mastery of the highest mysteries it has never been able to repeat. Personally, though, I've always had a soft spot for *22 Acacia Avenue (The continuing story of Charlotte the Harlot)*, the best romantic tale ever told to a background of drums and staccato guitar riffs. I've spent more than one afternoon walking down the Paseo de Acacias in Madrid, thinking of Charlotte who, according to Iron Maiden, you can go and visit whenever you feel down and lonely, which is the most frequent and least unstable state of modern man.

Finally, there's Yazoo. As far as I know, in the short time they put up with one another, Vince Clarke and Alison Moyet gave birth to two LPs under this name. The second LP is a final agony just meant to make money and shouldn't concern anybody. The first, *Upstairs at Eric's*, is simply spectacular. For years I listened to it every day, until a small but significant piece of my soul was locked away in each of those tracks.

The soul is the sum of all the things a person experiences before they become a sceptical bastard. "Don't Go", the first song, contains the euphoria of my naïve youthful drinking bashes, when I always felt strong and optimistic; "Too Pieces", the spring nights I used to spend watching the clouds lit up by the moon (one night I saw someone up there, I swear, although, either through lack of chance or patience, it never happened again). "Bad Connection" represents the hardship of all my inevitable separations. Woven into the burnt-velvet strains of Alison's voice, "Midnight" encloses the voluptuous serenity of summer nights, when summer nights existed and when they were voluptuous. For me, "In My Room" evokes the long hours spent alone in my bedroom, where I learnt almost everything I know about my fellow human beings. "Only You" encompasses the end of what had begun with Schubert's Piano Trio. And it was with "Tuesday" that I had the first premonition of how one fails at life in general. But I wasn't afraid, because "Winter Kills" made me take a liking to the somber tranquillity of defeat.

Clarke's lyrics are fairly incoherent and Moyet's are sometimes inscrutable. But in this case I think they serve to explain why that night, that same Friday night when I first exchanged words with Rosana, it was "Winter Kills" I chose to listen to:

You grew sunblind
You thought me unkind
To remind you how winter kills

The first time I listened to those words I was fifteen, like Rosana. Back then the parks and the slow hours of the sunset used to belong to me, too. I'm not looking for someone to absolve me, but I hope that someone can understand that I let myself grow sunblind, forgetting that winter would kill everything I cared about. If you think about it, it's not that bad when something a person has yearned for disappears. There was once a very talented homosexual in Lisbon who played at changing his name and he wrote it both quickly and definitively, perhaps on the back of a bill of exchange: you only have what you have already lost.

That night I had a dream. Before I go on, it might be worthwhile explaining that when I say I had a dream this shouldn't be taken the way it normally is. For almost everyone, when they say they've had a dream, it's like saying they've just farted. It's partly something improper and partly something no more important than that. For me, it's different. I have an enormous respect for dreams and I've always had it, or to be precise, I've had it since I was little more than a baby.

When I wasn't quite three I had a series of fevers that caused me to have terrifying hallucinations. My first memory, even before my mother's face or my father's voice, is one of those nightmares. In my dream it was stiflingly hot and my arms and legs were being devoured by a bale of tortoises. Put in those terms it seems a bit of a joke, but it scared the living daylights out of me. So much so that, according to my parents, the first thing I did once I was better and could go downstairs and play in the garden again was to bite the head off my little friend Roberto's tortoise, the only representative of that species I had ever seen and which must have inspired that terrible dream sequence.

After that I went on accumulating other memories and other nightmares, less primitive, but much more terrifying. Between the ages of four and eight I dreamt almost every night that my parents had died. The dream would vary, *ma non troppo*, in which it was simply other people who told me this had happened and I would grieve for awhile until my mother and father appeared safe and sound. There was also a *fortissimo* variation, in which my parents were sadistically executed in front of me and then I would be tortured for hours with the mocking account of the lack of strength and courage my father had shown before they finished him off. When I woke up, I would feel a sense of abandonment and contempt for my father that sometimes stayed with me until midday.

In puberty, coinciding with the outbreak of all that hormonal business, my dreams took on an ephemeral but encouraging slant. I started to dream about abandoned castles, impenetrable forests, strange houses with myriad rooms. This in itself wasn't particularly stimulating, but on exploring these places I almost always came across a series of delightful young (or not so young) ladies with whom I usually starred in lyrical scenes. From time to time we would just start fucking without further ado—why deny it? The good thing about both options was that they were willing to do whatever I wanted, things which the female I longed for at that moment refused to do: some would listen politely to my sweet compliments (not with rapture but with indulgence, which is a much more humane and useful thing), caressing me with their snow-white hands; others were tireless sluts and would take it however I wanted. Those dreams made reality unnecessary, and it's partly due to them that I don't complain about not having scored with anybody during my adolescence. Furthermore, I'm of the opinion that actual teenage love affairs are unbearably corny, while those who remain frustrated develop magnificent psychological shortcomings that will later delay the inevitable moment when having a screw is like lugging a sandbag up to a tenth floor apartment with your ankles tied together.

Once I reached adulthood and as part of the systematic amputation this state represents, my dreams started to become less frequent, until they almost ceased completely. This brings us back to what I was saying before. When I met Rosana, and when I dreamed of her that night, it was more than unusual for me to have had a dream, or at least one I still remembered in the morning. And that had increased the intensity of events in this area of my life. The nightmares I had in those days were so ghastly that I had to hold myself down tightly so as not to lose my marbles. If it was a dream about lovey-dovey little girls, it would leave me really quite upset, and when I woke up and discovered that the young lady had vanished I would become anxious and sink into an uncontrollably bad mood. In any case, it was always disturbing and I found it harder every time to shake it off and consume my daily portion of shit.

The strange thing about that night, and which might explain what came later, was that the young girl didn't disappear. Not immediately.

The dream took place in a hypermarket. I think it is the first and last time I've dreamed about a hypermarket. Although in fact it wasn't really a hypermarket, but one of those shopping centers with all different kinds of shops, bars, clubs, veterinary clinics, hairdressers, video stores, gyms, and also hypermarkets. It was a new shopping center and almost all the units were either empty or in the process of being occupied. Some—very few—shop windows were already full of merchandise, ready to attract and entrap the voracious *homo shopping*. One strange thing was that there were closed doors interspersed between the various shops that looked like front doors and harried people would occasionally go in or out of them, glancing around suspiciously.

I have no idea what I was doing there. I do know whom I was with: my sister and a group of her friends, four to be exact. The noteworthy thing about me being in such company is that I've never had a sister, unless there was some error or omission on my father's part. For this reason, the first thing that aroused my curiosity was my sister herself. This didn't last long. She had hair the same colour as mine and looked conventionally like me, that is, as much as sisters normally resemble their brothers. Brothers who look like their sisters generally do quite well out of it, but sisters who resemble their brothers tend to lose out by comparison. In short, after a few minutes, once the novelty wore off, my sister ceased to be of interest to me. As we walked away, she was chatting to one of her friends, whose face and way of walking suggested she also had a brother she resembled.

The other girls were a completely different kettle of fish. One of them, tall and dark-skinned, moved like a cat. Another, shorter but also dark-skinned, walked grabbing onto my arm and whispering obscenities in my ear while her heaving bosom, almost bursting out of her top, bounced up and down before my eyes. The last one, who had been talking to catwoman, was, quite simply, Rosana. In my dream she was perhaps three or four years older than in real life, no more than eighteen or nineteen. She was barely an inch or two shorter than the other girl and next to her, Rosana's skin shone delicately pale. A detail that distinguished her from fifteen-year-old Rosana was the look in her eyes, hardened by some kind of eyelash make up that brought out the blue of her eyes very effectively.

We would stop in front of shops that were either ready to open or still being fitted out. They would have a look at the window displays and I would keep looking at what interested me, that is, the heaving bosom; and when its owner leant forward a bit, it detached itself of the fabric around the neckline and ran through the entire range of suggestive forms that a bosom on the loose can adopt. However, I felt a certain indifference. I won't pretend I didn't consider taking advantage of the fact it was a dream to tear her dress off without any hassle. But that shameless damsel didn't really turn me on. She was the most easily attainable and that decreased her value by quite a bit. In dreams you aspire to the maximum, even though you sometimes run out of time and are left with nothing, just like in fucking real life.

While we wandered from shop to shop, I still hadn't decided what the maximum was. I liked Rosana and the catwoman about equally and I was fairly confident I had enough time. However, the relative immobility of the dream, which basically consisted of moving slowly along a long corridor, didn't last long. Although I had at no point had the impression that we were heading for a specific place, when we arrived in front of one of the closed doors that seemed to be an entrance to a residential complex, my sister stopped abruptly and said, "Well, this might be it."

She took out a key and tried it on the door. The lock turned easily.

"This is it, then," said her friend who also had a brother.

A steep staircase was visible behind the door. My sister and her friend went up first and the four of us left followed a short while later. Rosana took the initiative and the busty one and I brought up the rear. At the top of the stairs was a small, dark living room. We made ourselves comfortable in a variety of chairs and sat in silence. They were all waiting for some sign from my sister. She was wringing her hands.

"We're not just going to sit here and wait until they decide to pay attention to us, are we?" the dark-skinned catwoman broke the silence.

"We don't have much choice," said my sister, "unless you have an idea?"

"Yes, I do. Of course I'm not waiting for anyone. Anyone who wants anything from me can come and find me. If they find me sitting here I know what they're going to think, and I'm not prepared to put up with that. I'm going to take a look around."

The dark girl got up and smoothed down her dress. It was a summery lilac robe.

"Maybe no one will come looking for you," my sister warned her.

"Perhaps," the other girl replied, leaving the room.

My sister looked bewildered for a moment. Then she composed herself and asked, "What are the rest of you going to do?"

"I'm staying here with you," her sidekick set the tone.

"I'm in no hurry" said the busty one with a smile, pinching my arm.

Nobody else was in a hurry or felt like answering. My sister looked at Rosana and me, urging us on. In the end she insisted, "What about you two?"

Rosana sighed and then let her words drop into my sister's embarrassing failure: "I'm getting out of here as well. Not right now, later. When it doesn't look like I've left with her."

It was my turn. The dream had changed so much and I didn't have a clue what they were talking about. I suspected that my sister would prefer me to say I'd stay, and the busty one took it for granted. I also realized that I was of very little interest to Rosana. I saw only one way out. I stood up and said forcefully, "I choose to go. Right now, as if I were going after her. To find her."

The four of them sat there looking at me, incredulous, although Rosana less so than the other three.

"What a poor idiot," mumbled my sister, turning away. "And I'm sure you're thinking she wants you to find her."

"It's not a case of thinking anything, but of finding out. If it turns out she doesn't, I'll give up and come back."

"Don't waste your time," said big tits resentfully. "He knows what he needs. Perhaps she'll feel sorry for him and they'll think they're happy. Good luck, sweetheart."

I left the room and started to explore the house. Its size was nothing like other houses I'd seen, the stunted offspring of real estate speculation. I walked through dozens of rooms, passages, flights of stairs, halls that led to other halls, basements, attics. It was a colossal labyrinth that spread in all directions, although it might be worth pointing out that none of its constituent parts was too big, which prevented you from gaining any sense of perspective. Besides, none of it was that well-lit.

After about approximately half an hour of searching, I was startled by the sound of something falling in one of the rooms. I inspected the room and saw a picture frame that had fallen over on top of a sideboard. Not far away was a small black cat, barely more than a kitten. The animal was motionless and I was struck by its eyes, not yellow as you might expect in a black cat, but a pale violet, almost lilac colour. Like my sister's friend's dress, I remembered.

I slowly approached it and reached out to pick it up. It didn't resist. On the contrary, it snuggled up to me and gave me four or five quick licks on the back of my hand with its little pink tongue. With the cat in my arms, I continued my exploration of the house. While I examined the series of deserted rooms, the cat played with my fingers and in particular with my thumb, probably fascinated by its size. At the end of a corridor, after a long period of silence and with only the cat for company, a feminine voice stopped me.

"Wait."

I turned round and saw Rosana. Her pale, almost white hair, made her stand out immediately from the shadows. I waited. Very soon after she was at my side.

"What are you carrying?"

"A kitten. It was all alone here."

"A black cat."

"You're superstitious?"

"No. Let me hold it."

I gave it to her and she took it by the scruff of the neck.

The little animal was left dangling from her hand like a hanged man. Then she ran over to a window, opened it and viciously threw it out.

"You've killed it," I said, astonished.

"I'm not so sure. Cats fall on their feet, but we're quite high up. I might have."

"It hadn't done anything to you."

"No, not to me," she admitted, pointing at my hand. I looked at it. My thumb was bloody and the skin was torn.

"It wasn't hurting," I exclaimed.

"It always does later, when there's nothing you can do about it. Was it a cat you were looking for?"

"What about you?"

"I was just walking around. I saw you and wanted to check on you. I won't bother you anymore. See you later."

Rosana brought her cheek close to mine and pretended to give me a chaste kiss, as a sister's friend might. However, halfway through she changed it into something much more lascivious. She pulled back a bit and waited for my reaction. I didn't move.

"Shall I go or shall I stay?" she said.

"Don't be in such a hurry."

She did the same thing several times, with more saliva each time. She tasted of fruit and smiled as if she were up to mischief. I tried to embrace her, but she always wriggled away from me. In the end I managed to grasp her shoulders. They were smooth and warm, they felt soft as if there were no bones underneath.

"I like your shoulders," I confessed.

"Your sister would tell you off if she heard you. She doesn't like me. And I'm sure she wouldn't approve of this."

I opened her blouse and let my fingers explore what was beneath it. Rosana didn't put up any resistance. She looked at herself and then at me, amused.

"She'd be even more disapproving of what you're doing now."

I had a moment of doubt. It was wrong. What I was doing was truly wrong. My sister was the yardstick who measured all I did and this would be way off scale. Rosana was making fun of my sister, and I was her accomplice, maybe even the instigator. Rosana had nothing to do with my sister, but, whether I liked it or not, I did. I hesitated. Then she, Rosana, made the decision for me. She went and closed the door, then took her blouse off completely, revealing her slim girl's torso in all its glory. My sister was a sad, repressed creature. Rosana was happy and carefree. I had only a single reservation: "Tell me that you want this because of me, not to get back at my sister."

Rosana burst out laughing. As she took off her skirt she reassured me, "You're so funny. I don't give a damn about your sister."

I'm more or less a gentleman and nobody should expect a detailed account of what took place between me and Rosana in that room. She was compliant and tireless and I was as unscrupulous as the situation demanded. I will only describe the last thing I saw before I woke up: my sister was standing in the doorway with a horrified expression on her face; Rosana greeted her and then carried on shamelessly, the look of callous, childish joy never once leaving her face. And I, the man, saw that everything was good.

At eleven a.m. on the dot, my old body, struggling to recover from alcoholic over-indulgence and a dream about Rosana, was sitting on the bench we had agreed on the day before. Memories of the elusive Rosana I had dealt with in the evening and the shady lady who had unexpectedly made me so happy during the night swirled around in my mind. Surrounded by old people, mothers, children and small dogs, I played at betting with myself which of the two Rosanas would turn up that morning, if either of them turned up at all. A bookmaker would never have risked his money on anyone turning up for my date, and if there was some pressing reason for him to take the bet, he would never have expected a Rosana any different from the day before. In short, a bookmaker would have fulfilled his fate, which is not to win, just as it is not a doctor's fate to cure anyone. The fate of the bookmaker is that one who doesn't know better will get rich at his expense while he earns little more than a modest return. The doctor's fate is for his science to succumb when faced with one of the meticulous agents of death. And mine, though it has nothing to do with that of bookmakers or doctors, was an unforeseeably wicked Rosana.

However, when quarter past eleven came around, and my electronic slave of a wristwatch informed me of it with one of its stupid bleeps, I was still as single as the malt whisky to which I owed the pounding in my temples. The only thing a man can give, at least those of us who don't have any outsize moral or physical attributes compared to others, is his word, and the only thing I could do when my watch told me the time was to get up and walk away with dignity. So this is what I did. I straightened my tie (not the one Rosana had praised the day before, but more or less similar in style) and I turned my steps towards one of the park exits.

She let me walk fifty or sixty feet. All of a sudden she appeared from behind a tree.

"Hi there, cop."

I stopped to admire her. She had chosen a daring sporty outfit for the occasion, knee length stretch pants and a spaghetti strap tank top glued to every part of her body above her waist, her shoulders almost intolerably bare. She had her hair tied up in a kind of bun, which made her look slightly older.

"I was just leaving," I said.

"So soon? You didn't even wait an extra minute. We women always arrive late."

"I don't wait for women. My religion doesn't allow me to. So I'm off," I started walking again and stopped midway, "unless you beg me to stay, of course."

Rosana gave me a sideways glance.

"Unless I beg you? On your way then, I can see what your weak spot is."

"What is it then?"

"It's easy to spot your weak spot," she joked, "It's the same as those who hang around the school railings to look at girls' panties."

"If that's what you think, then let's call it a day, Rosana. You're very cute but you don't know when the wind is blowing your way. I couldn't care less about underwear."

Then I started to walk with every intention of not stopping until I received some definite sign from her that she was willing to play the game. It was the moment of truth for the punter and that wicked little girl put an end to any uncertainty with a sole hammer blow.

"Good," she shouted, "I'm not wearing any."

"What?"

"Panties. I'm not wearing any panties." As I made my way back she explained, "You can see everything through these leggings. There's nothing uglier than going round showing the world that you're being wedgied by your underwear."

I must confess that, like any other dirty swine, my eyes went immediately to check the most obvious part of Rosana's anatomy, to see if she was telling the truth. And she was, in an obvious and disturbing way.

"Watch it, cop. That's pushing it a bit," she warned, folding her hands in front of her. There's no need for me to explain my confusion. It was so great that Rosana must have felt obliged to help me out.

"It's a deal" she said, coming closer.

"What's a deal?"

"I beg you. Please don't go. So come and sit with me."

"I'm not sure I'm going to keep the deal," I tried to back out. "I think you're getting mixed up in all this. You must be too young. How old are you?"

Rosana turned flirty as she answered, "Right now I'm fifteen. Sixteen in January. Are you old enough to be my father?"

"No. I wasn't socializing with women when you were born. I only loved them."

"The way you talk is really funny."

"I'm a very funny cop. That's why I work with juvenile delinquents."

"Have you caught Borja yet?"

"I'm not after Borja. I'm interested in his pusher. Borja is a hopeless moron, with a father who chairs the Alumni Association and gives him fifteen thousand pesetas pocket money every Saturday. If we put all the morons like him, or his father, in jail, we'd run out of prisons."

Rosana walked back towards a bench and sat down. I didn't move.

"Are you really sure you don't want to come and sit with me?" she invited me. "Everyone wants to sit with me, if I let them. I'm very popular."

"I don't doubt it at all. You're first in your class and the prettiest girl in school. If you had a ton of pimples and your ass was so big you couldn't get your leggings on you'd be less popular, even if you were top of the class. But it's not such a bad thing that you take advantage of it. No-one would feel sorry for you if you didn't take advantage of it."

"Come here," she insisted, patting the bench with her lily white hand.

"I shouldn't. You were late. If I sit down you'll think it doesn't matter whether or not you comply with my conditions."

"I promise I won't."

"You promise. And what makes you think that's good enough for me? I've lied a thousand times when I've made promises."

Her full lips, ever so slightly redder than normal, quirked up in a triumphant crescent moon.

"I've been here since ten to eleven. Behind that tree. I'm not lying. I saw you arrive at eleven o'clock exactly and set the alarm on your watch."

"Alright," I agreed. "You like to set traps for me. You have a twisted mind. Just the type of girl I like."

I sat down next to her and as I was taking my seat I had a very foolish, very sentimental idea. In the course of my love life, in spite of what I expected when I was twenty and all the girls used to laugh at me, I've managed to enjoy the favors of some really quite not so bad looking women. But I never had the sensation of fulfilling a desire, that is that the little thing sitting quiet and docile at one's side is the object of desire you've been looking for and has evaded you a thousand times. The most I got to experience was a feeling that I'd robbed someone of their desire, like when I conquered Sabine, a magnificent German girl the guy who had been my best friend until that day had been lusting after. This can serve as a substitute to temporarily shore up your vanity. But in the long run, it's completely useless. Well anyway, when I saw myself sitting there, part of a duo whose other half consisted of Rosana, who was welcoming me with her mischievous sweetness, I realized that I was fulfilling my own desire for the first time ever, a true and eternal one. I already know it sounds tremendous bullshit. I even had goosepimples.

Rosana had turned thoughtful.

"I get five thousand pesetas pocket money on Saturdays," she suddenly confessed. "Do you think my dad's an idiot too?"

Perhaps because I was feeling vulnerable and tender, I decided to be brutal, forgetting that the girl next to me was not yet sweet sixteen.

"Of course he is. There are women who have to give some stinking drunk a blow job to earn five thousand pesetas. This way you'll never know the value of things."

Rosana's eyes shone.

"Was your father poor?"

"My father *is* poor, if by that you mean someone who has to work and then pay taxes on every last fucking peseta he earns. That's what I think, anyway."

"So you're a socialist."

"Who told you that?"

"My father says that poor people are socialists because socialists promise them that they're going to take everything from those of us who aren't poor."

"Your father is really very confused."

"What are you then?"

"I'm a Bolshevik," I improvised.

"And what do Bolsheviks want?"

"You wouldn't understand."

Rosana frowned.

"Try me. I'm not stupid. And I studied twentieth century history in eighth grade."

We Bolsheviks go back to the nineteenth century, not the twentieth. We want to shoot people like your father and then shoot poor people so they realize that we're all crooks and no-one is worth saving."

"You're kidding. You're laughing at me."

"Of course I am. I'm a nobody, and I'll stop being whatever I am if you ask me to."

"You're nuts, cop."

"Not at all. I've got my opinion about what the shit going round in people's heads is worth. Not a single drop of your tears, gorgeous."

She was confused, and I was diving into her clear blue gaze with more enthusiasm than a thirty-something year-old guy ought to show towards a fifteen year-old girl on a public park bench. She avoided my eyes and wrapped her arms around one of her legs. This was not a trivial detail. For those legs I would have been capable of letting my Argentine dentist lecture me, putting my glass rubbish in the correct recycling bin, or even wearing a cellphone clipped to my waistband.

"Is that a compliment?" she asked.

"I don't pay compliments. I declare my love or I get the hell out."

For a moment it seemed like she was blushing, but it must have been a mirage. She untied her hair and observed me, her chin resting on her delicate fist.

"Today's tie isn't as nice as yesterday's."

"I'll take it off if it bothers you."

"Okay."

I unknotted my tie, folded it and put it in the inside pocket of my jacket.

"Better now?"

"Yes. You're not as old as I thought. You don't have wrinkles round your neck."

"I don't have wrinkles anywhere. But I do have a few gray hairs."

"They don't really show."

"I don't mind if they show. The two most ridiculous things a man can do is use hair growth restorer and dye his gray hairs. Does your father dye his?"

"My father's as bald as an egg."

"Of course, I should have guessed. And what does your father do?"

"He's an architect."

"What about your mother?"

"My mother doesn't do anything. She plays the piano and speaks French. I think that's all she knows how to do."

"Your mother has time to get bored, Rosana. You should always respect someone with time to get bored. That's how people grow wise."

Rosana shook her head.

"Not my mother. Sometimes not even the maid takes her seriously."

"I'm beginning to like your mother. I get on better with unlucky people."

"I'm lucky."

"You're something else. Do you have any brothers or sisters?"

"Five. They're all older than me, married with kids and all that. Except for Sonsoles. She's the eldest, but she's single. My brother Pablo says she's been left on the shelf. She gets angry when he says that."

There was a cruel indifference towards Sonsoles in Rosana's tone of voice. I did some digging. "Do you get on well with your sister?"

"With Sonsoles? She's too much of a smart aleck to get along with anyone. She never does anything wrong and she thinks everyone around her are idiots. By all accounts she's forever rubbing her colleagues at the Ministry up the wrong way. She does it to my mother too, and even my father."

"What about you?"

Rosana put the leg she had tucked up on the bench back down and stretched both legs out in front of her. Comparing them with Sonsoles' scrawny sticks it was hard to believe they were related. "Sonsoles knows I'm not an idiot," she replied maliciously.

"For any specific reason?"

"Sisters have secrets … "

"I won't ever tell her. I don't know her and I don't intend to."

She stared at me, as if giving me an X-ray.

"I'll keep your secret," I promised.

"It was just after I turned thirteen. At that time Sonsoles had a suitor. A guy with a belly and a moustache. I'm glad you don't have a belly or a moustache. I thought that all policemen had moustaches."

"Those are the Guardia Civil. Were."

"Well this guy was a lawyer or something like that, but he had one anyway. They both came to our summer house in Llanes. One day I was in my room changing after a trip to the beach when I saw him in the garden, spying on me. I'd already stripped off and he'd already seen me, so I took my time. I got dressed as if nothing was wrong and went downstairs to eat. At dinner the guy was so laid back, calling Sonsoles *darling*. I ate the starter and main course without saying a word. When they brought dessert I snapped at my sister that another summer she should bring a boyfriend who wouldn't go behind her back. At first Sonsoles didn't understand, then she told me to shut up. But I said that Mr. Moustache liked younger girls. Then Sonsoles got really mad and my father sent me out of the room, but the guy had already turned bright red and on my way out I took the chance to advise him that next time he wanted to watch me undressing he should either hide himself better or ask my permission. The lawyer left first thing next morning and my sister hated me, but she never again thought I was an idiot."

From what she'd told me I could imagine everything: the lawyer drenched in sweat in the undergrowth, his hairy legs bowed under the weight of his hideous paunch; Rosana slowly getting dressed and pretending not to notice; Sonsoles' fussiness at first and then being shown up by her not-so-charming prince's sticky onanism.

The child her parents had unfortunately given her as a sister had turned out to be her worst enemy, a walking humiliation which served to pay for all her sins. It was a perfect twist of fate: to make her live under the same roof with a child who had exactly what she lacked, the ability to charm others. I imagined all her efforts to hide how much she hated her, going to pick her up from school, taking her shopping, telling her secrets and sharing confidences. For the first time I felt sorry for her, sorry for that bitch Sonsoles.

"A nice little story," I observed. "Especially for the pig with the moustache. He must have had a great time huddled in the bushes."

"Don't you believe it. I was only a child then. It wasn't a big deal."

"You were?"

"My bikini fits much better now."

"I wouldn't mind seeing that."

She smiled. She had a knockout smile, with dimples and all and her teeth were absolutely perfect.

"That's what I like about you."

"What?"

"The fact you don't hide in the garden like the jerk with the moustache. You would have asked my permission to watch, bold as brass."

"We Bolsheviks aren't allowed to hide. Our beliefs don't allow it. What isn't, isn't and what is, is there for all to see."

"Do you want to see me in my bikini?"

"I already told you that."

"Take me to the swimming pool."

"Now?"

"This afternoon. I always go to the pool with my girlfriends on Saturdays. My parents don't have to know I'm going with you, and if we go to a different one my friends won't find out either."

"It's been years since I've been to a swimming pool in Madrid. I don't even know where there is one."

"Well, find out. That's what cops are for."

There was something strange about the way she'd said that, and something even stranger about the way I came to the conclusion that I had to tell her what I told her next.

"If I'm going to take you to a swimming pool, there's something I need to tell you."

"What?"

"I'm not a cop."

"I'd already worked that out."

"I'm not a maniac either."

"Aha."

"It's as if you didn't care."

"Of course I do. What're you called? Really."

"Jaime," I lied.

"I liked Javier better. But I like you better than the cop. So, are you going to take me to the swimming pool or not?"

"Yes, if you want me to," I gave in.

"Yes, I do. Pick me up here at half past four. Now I'm going to work up a bit of a sweat. They think I've gone out for a run. *Ciao.*"

She went running off, her hair blowing in the wind, and I was left trying to unravel something confused about Dante and Beatrice and heaven and hell and the fucking certainty that no pain could be worse than remembering happy times when you're down on your luck.

Going to the swimming pool always reminds me of my childhood. And that doesn't mean that going to the swimming pool makes me happy. In spite of what thousands of simpletons maintain (perhaps in their eagerness to recoup the physical and psychological effort that having children entails), children live in an uncivilized and morally inferior world. Abuse, violence and gratuitous cruelty reign amongst them. One of the few things I appreciate about being an adult is that I don't have to be constantly afraid that people who are taller than me might decide to send me sprawling to the ground and twist my arm until I burst into tears. It might happen on very rare occasions, but in the school playground it's very rare that it doesn't happen. In school playgrounds it's always the biggest brute who rules the roost, and the rest, among whom there may be highly spiritual children or precocious talents, have to resign themselves to doing his coarse bidding or become martyrs, or perhaps becoming martyrs in spite of having done his bidding, depending on how bad a mood the relevant beast is in. In childhood, the crudest and most brutal characteristics of humanity prevail. When I was a child surrounded by other children, I used to hate the human race and regretted having landed among members of such a dangerous and primitive species. I don't exactly consider myself a philanthropist nowadays, but the adult riffraff, who form the backdrop to my daily life, sometimes offer the counterpoint of exhibiting a certain intellectual merit. I may be mistaken, but I prefer Lorenzo de' Medici to a bully with his shirt tails hanging out, his shoelaces undone and a dirty face, beating his chest surrounded by a group of intimidated little kids.

I had a powerful opportunity to experience the fact that childhood is a state at odds with intelligence, sensitivity and all the other characteristics that differentiate man from other primates thanks to the one and only time when I was about to believe the opposite. When I was seven or eight years old, I managed to get the dumbest boy in school, an individual capable of fighting eight other boys at once and beating them all, to blindly obey any orders I gave him. For a while, I lived under the illusion of submitting brute force to the plans of a superior mind. In this way, my circle of friends, who did not partake in the sterile pastimes that occupied most children but instead preferred the practice of all sorts of industrious activities (like making explosives, constructing miniature cities and organizing fantastic storytelling competitions), were able to dedicate themselves to them without wasting time fighting with other boys. When anyone tried to bother us, I would set Lisardo (that was my invincible slave's name) loose on them and he would deal with the troublemakers comprehensively, breaking noses, fracturing skulls and knocking out teeth like a veritable war machine. Such was my control over him that after each scuffle Lisardo would sing a little ditty of my invention that combined his name and surnames with the word "willy". The result was grotesque, and Lisardo himself was the first to raucously applaud it.

Anyway, one day when Lisardo seemed a bit surly, I took the unfortunate step of submitting my power over him to a test from which it didn't come out well, and which convinced me to watch out for tall guys for the rest of my childhood. Nobody had attacked us and so there was no reason for Lisardo to sing his little song. But, to impress the others, I ordered him to sing. Lisardo seemed reluctant. I began to sing it to encourage him. The giant looked at me and I realized, too late, that something was stirring, perhaps for the first time, inside his thick skull. Without a word he came over to me, lifted me up in the air and gave me a tremendous beating, right there, in front of everyone. I can still feel the blows and my reputation, based for the most part on my influence over Lisardo, was completely destroyed. Ever since, I've never believed that a child will respect any authority except that of whoever can hit harder than he can. Everything else is a waste of time.

Another thing that puts me off swimming pools is that there, the suntanned airheads who do somersaults off the diving board are at the top of the food-chain. I've never been able to get a suntan and I've always been loath to accept that the best thing to do with your skull is risk smashing it to bits against the end of the board or the side of the pool. As a consequence, swimming pools have never been a place I've had much success in. To tell you the truth, my life at swimming pools has been for the most part a life of silence and solitude. One of the few activities that helped me while away the time at swimming pools, other than swimming and going on reconnaissance walks, was reading. Even though it takes all sorts, I prefer to do those three things best silently and by myself.

The swimming pool was the place where hot chicks were hotter than anywhere else: the problem was that they were always fawning over the kings of the diving board and didn't even see the sallow-complexioned peasants like me. This developed my imagination and gave me a complex soul, for which, as I believe I've written in these very pages, I am not ungrateful, but the price of all this was a certain sadness I didn't much enjoy at the time. When I got tired of my book (which happened frequently since a pool is a pretty uncomfortable place to read a book) and I got tired of swimming (which was even easier since swimming physically tires you out) and I got tired of walking around (inebriated by all the suntanned flesh on display that sooner or later would fall under the sporty caresses of the springboard kings), I had no place left to hide. At that point I would go and sit at the edge of the pool and twilight would fall, and twilight was in a way a luke-warm type of humiliation.

With all this in mind, and for other reasons that I am neither willing nor able of summarising, I experienced a mixture of curiosity and unease on thinking about the possibility of going to a swimming pool with Rosana that Saturday. My curiosity was piqued by the idea of not being alone at the swimming pool, but in the company of Rosana. My childhood aside, from time to time I've been to a swimming pool with someone, but never with somebody like her, whom, although she wasn't as tanned as her sister Sonsoles, I could identify with the girls who used to ignore me in my younger years. The unease sprang from the prospect of returning to that world I had always found so hostile, full of diving boards and guys whose complexions were invariably less pale than mine. Sure, you can meditate to your heart's content to try to come to terms with what makes you different, even to turn it into a source of pride. After all, who doesn't try to overcome their shortcomings by turning them into a virtue? That's all fine and dandy, but sometimes, when you're least expecting it, it slowly dawns on you that one of the biggest wimps in history, that ungainly Czech called Franz Kafka, told the tale of a poor bloke who turns into a cockroach one morning and is rejected by his family, who go off on a daytrip when the cockroach finally dies. As is well known, two of the things we featherless bipeds most desire is not to be rejected by anybody and that nobody should go off on a daytrip after we die.

At four-thirty, give or take a minute, I arrived at the park bench where we had agreed to meet and found Rosana already waiting for me with her swimming bag and her beautiful, disturbing little face. She was wearing a short, printed dress, one of those dresses where the waistline is really high, starting just under the curve of the bust. When she got up from the bench to greet me, I realized exactly how short it was when I saw for the first time her naked legs up to the middle of her thighs. Although admittedly younger and much more fascinating, she was the girl from the holiday ads you never come across when you decide to go on holiday somewhere with a beach, where there is always an abundance of less dazzling options, more abundant and less dazzling the nearer it is to the end of the month and the further from the last pay packet. It's not like the most important thing in life is to be with beautiful women, but it is true that when you hang out with a beautiful woman you tend to admit more freely that someone up there's looking out for you. It's an unavoidable, base genetic or biochemical phenomenon for which there is no need to feel personally responsible.

"Have you decided which pool we're going to?" was Rosana's eager greeting, as she swung her torso from left to right.

"I've had a look. There's one near the Ciudad Universitaria campus. I think I went there once when I was a student. It's a long way from here. I don't think your girlfriends would go there."

"What did you study?"

"Philosophy."

"Are you a philosopher?"

"No, just the opposite. I work in a bank."

"That sounds great, surrounded by dough all day."

"I don't get to see the dough. I add it up, multiply it and divide it. That's all I do now, although I once wrote a thesis on Leibniz."

"On who?"

"Nobody. He's much less important than James Dean, for example. If anyone ever talks to you about Leibniz, you can forget it. Knowing who he is won't be at all useful. It's not done me any good. Shall we go?"

We crossed the park and went to pick up my cousin's car. It would have to answer my transport requirements until the following Wednesday, according to the random estimation that, somewhat put out by my demands, the clodhopper who ran the garage where I'd left my own car had given me. A guy who, from what I'd seen and heard during our little chat, didn't need to know anything about Leibniz, James Dean, or the correlation between customer service and the level of demand for car repairs.

"My, what a small car you've got," declared Rosana.

I was on the verge of saying it wasn't mine, that my car had a sixteen valve engine and ABS and alloy wheel rims all standard features nowadays in any proper car (which mine was, in fact), but not in my cousin's. It's incredible what a jerk a person can become, just because they have a few credit cards in their wallet, I told myself. I said, "The only big thing some people have is their car. Not me, that's not my style."

Rosana made herself comfortable in the passenger seat and resignedly wound down the window. She didn't complain about this, or the lack of air conditioning, or the absence of a flashy stereo system. She was an angel, after all.

We crossed a conveniently deserted Madrid. We went first up and then down the Gran Vía, Rosana telling me little things about her family, related to the fact that the swimming pool was near the university campus.

"My brothers and sisters all went to university. All the boys are engineers of some kind. Leticia is a doctor and Sonsoles studied law. But she's not a lawyer because she passed the civil service entrance exams. Sonsoles was the best student. Distinctions in everything."

"The Law School was opposite my faculty," I told her. "I knew some girls who must have been a bit like your sister. They used to take notes in perfectly rounded handwriting and underlined things with coloured pens. They could hold ten different coloured pens in one hand at the same time. They knew everything by heart and they wouldn't have known what to say if someone asked them the difference between statutory rape and leasehold."

"What is the difference?"

I'd repeated the line I'd picked up from an old friend who'd studied Law, without thinking what I was saying and especially that I was saying *rape*. It was an inappropriate term to use in that situation, to say the least. However, I decided to carry on as if nothing were amiss, hoping that Rosana didn't know what it meant and that it wouldn't cross her mind to look it up. I delivered the punchline my old friend always used to use: "For statutory rape you need cunning but for a leasehold you need money."

Rosana seemed lost in thought and I didn't like it. She finally shared the conclusion she'd reached. "The problem here is that I'm much more cunning than you. You'll have to pay me somehow."

I had no option but to play along. "I can't afford to pay much."

"I'll give you a discount. Or, better yet, I'll make you rob a bank. Wicked women always make honest men rob banks or steal the worker's monthly wages. Honest men are left to wallow in despair, while wicked women disappear into the sunset with handsome scoundrels who beat them up."

"Where did a girl your age learn all these things? I can't believe it's just from watching TV."

"I listen to people talking and once in awhile I read a book. It's easy to find out what adults don't want you to know. I read *The Complete Encyclopaedia of Married Life* when I was ten. I was curious as to why it was on top shelf of the bookshelf. I balanced two chairs on top of each other and found out why. I used to find all that stuff a bit disgusting until one day I remembered the pictures and then it didn't seem so gross. I also know where my father keeps his dirty money. First I had to work out that it wasn't called dirty money because it was covered with filth or something but that it was money that daddy takes out of his company illegally. Aren't you going to ask me where it is?"

"I don't really care about your father's money, dirty or laundered. I'm sorry to disappoint you. Perhaps you thought I was a thief."

"No, you don't look like one. But just in case."

I had worked out in advance that Rosana would pay a reduced entry, not out of stinginess, but due to some kind of belated scruple. But from the age of fourteen you can't tell the difference, or rather, they all have to pay full price. It was stupid and it was no consolation because God would either approve the fact that I was more than twice her age and there would be nothing to worry about or he would not and I in that case I was in deep shit even if I managed to get a waiver from the Vatican. But I consoled myself that at least she was old enough to pay full price at the swimming pool.

We separated after the ticket office. Rosana went into the ladies' changing room and I went into the men's, with its permanent smell of ripe feet and rancid sweat, two of the many undesirable side effects of sport activities and poor hygiene. I was wearing my trunks under my trousers so I rushed through that revolting place as quickly as I could, dodging the puddles that splattered the floor. The lawns on the other side were not too crowded. I waited for ten minutes or so and Rosana appeared, in her bikini.

There have been various high points in my wretched existence. One was a Christmas when I was given two

Madelman action figures: the deep sea diver and his arch-enemy, the black pirate. The highlight of my teenage years was in my last year of High School when I finished my final biology exam and we burned all our books and notes along with an effigy of the teacher. The highlight of the rest of my life was the afternoon when Rosana appeared before my eyes, as if coming out from a shell that had just floated up from beneath the waves. She looked more like Botticelli's Venus than ever, although thinner, less fleshy, since Venuses in Botticelli's day ate great chunks of lard and whatever junk food there was at the time, instead of low-fat yoghurt. If I make an effort, I can remember that her bikini was pink and that I hadn't done anything to deserve her. I've always been of the opinion that the best and most valuable things in life are those you don't deserve. Things you deserve are too imbued with your sense of self and are totally useless.

"How do I look?" her crystal voice tinkled.

"Do you want the truth?"

"That's why I asked."

"I understand how your sister's boyfriend felt. But you already know that. Does the name Botticelli ring a bell?"

"No. Should it?"

"Not necessarily. In another life you forced him to include you in all his paintings. But if you remember all the people who love you, you won't have any room left for your own thoughts."

"You'll make me big headed."

"You already are, but you're right to be. One day you won't be as pretty as you are now and you'll have cancer and you won't be able to believe anything anyone tells you."

"That's spooky."

"Carpe diem. If Garcilaso de la Vega prettifies it everyone thinks it's a nice idea. If you describe it exactly how it is, they say you are spooky."

"I studied Garcilaso in eighth grade."

"You studied everything in eighth grade."

"Not everything."

"Let's leave it. Sun or shade? I hate the sun."

"I don't mind. I haven't come here to get a tan."

We found a spot under a tree. Rosana spread out her towel and then stretched out on top of it. I took off my trousers but not my T-shirt and sat down on a folded towel.

"Do you go swimming in a T-shirt?" she asked.

"I don't think I'll swim. Swimming pools are full of piss and bacteria."

"Don't you like anything?"

"I like ice-skating and rhythmic gymnastics. Watching, not participating. I also like to sleep soundly, when I can. And I like you."

"Thanks. I like you too. It must be because you're not like Borja."

"It must be. But there could be other options. Have you ever seen one of those pumped up guys with slicked-back hair and a mint-green Burberry polo shirt who wear hi-tech watches like you'd wear if you were going deep-sea diving?"

"Nacho, Leticia's husband. He also likes skydiving. He always checks himself out whenever he sees a mirror."

"And?"

"He's a dick."

"You're not supposed to say things like that."

"I'm not supposed to go to the swimming pool with a stranger who is so much older than me and likes me so much," said Rosana, turning over lazily.

"Of course not. I didn't mean to correct you, you just surprised me. I like you better like this. I can't stand the little miss goody-two-shoes types."

"Everyone thinks I'm a good girl. At school I get prizes for good behaviour."

"All teachers are mentally atrophied. It comes from being surrounded by people who know less than them. They stick to the basics and don't even realize when their students start to know more than them. You must find school a waste of time."

"I have to study. I want to go to college."

"What will you study?"

"Business administration."

"It takes ages. Take my advice, save yourself all that bother, forget maths and exams and notes and become a top model, you're made for it. You'll be a millionaire while your girlfriends are still underlining their notes. Then hire someone to play the stock market for you, study the courses you best like and laugh at those poor sods slaving away, renting out their brain cells at so much an hour."

"Like you?"

"Yes, I rented out my brain cells. Now I don't know what I rent out any more, nor do I think about it."

Rosana sat up a bit. She lay on one side with her head resting on her hand as if she were in a swimsuit ad. I wasn't complaining.

"You must be some kind of executive," she said, "based on the tie you were wearing. I don't understand why you're not happy."

"Do I have to be?"

"Everyone wants to be an executive. Travelling, having a pretty secretary and expensive suits, earning loads of money."

I closed my eyes. I had ended up getting involved with a minor, I had taken her away from her neighborhood, I had managed to get her to take almost all her clothes off and instead of taking advantage of her by doing some other abominable act that would give me some release, which might fit the bill, there I was surrounded by families, talking to her about the ins and outs of my job. It didn't matter how, but I needed to put a stop to it.

"Look, Rosana," I started to explain. "I don't know what nonsense your father or someone else has been filling your head with. In my experience, travelling means getting on a plane to fly to another city where it's always either raining or cold. On the outward flight there are guys with dandruff and on the return flight there are guys with dandruff and who sweat non-stop. Sometimes you have to stay overnight in that rainy city and you zap through the forty satellite channels on TV three times before turning out the light and cursing the whole damn world. Expensive suits are nice in the beginning. Something one looks forward to, I'll admit it. And if you go to a den full of executives, as you call them, you'll see that the young ones are all wearing new, neatly ironed clothes. Almost all of them still live at home with mommy and enjoy her loving ministrations, or perhaps those of her maid. But if you look at those who already have a few gray hairs, who have surrendered to their fate, or rather to their wife or her maid, who are much less skilled and much less willing than mommy and her maid, you'll see that their suits are rumpled and shiny, their trousers show seven creases and their ties have stains on them. There's no point in buying more new suits. Before they realize, after about six months or so, they're done for and suits, like everything else, no longer matter. As for the money, the only person who can say he's loaded is the one who doesn't put up with any shit nor with other people's problems, unless they amuse him. Fun and work are incompatible. And there's no such thing as a sexy secretary who lasts more than two and a half months. Mine didn't even manage a week. My current one is about sixty and looks like Edward G. Robinson's twin sister."

"Who?"

"An actor. American. From a thousand years ago."

Rosana thought it over, but not for long.

"Well I'd like to be an executive," she insisted.

"You'll get bags under your eyes, your periods will go haywire and you won't be able to prevent your bosses being more interested in your ass than in your ideas. There's never time to weigh up an idea, but an ass can be weighed up quickly. The advantage of being a model is that you earn an honest living from your ass, without taking part in any silly farce."

"You're a male chauvinist pig."

"I'm observant, that's all. Why don't we talk about you? Thinking about my colleagues at work gives me a headache."

Rosana almost leapt to her feet.

"I'm going for a swim. Are you coming?"

"Why now, all of a sudden?"

"I'm hot. Are you coming or not?"

"Just to watch you."

We went over to the pool and Rosana dived straight in, tracing a flawless arc in the air. She swam front crawl perfectly, and this made me rather envious because I'd swum thousands of miles but no more than a couple of lengths of crawl in my entire life because it wore me out and I got water in my ears. At first I stood waiting. When she turned into her sixth length it occurred to me that it might be a good idea to find somewhere to sit in the shade. She swam more than thirty lengths without stopping or lessening the pace she had established at the start. She finally climbed out and walked over to where I was. Dripping wet, muscles tensed from the exercise, her body was even more of a shock. The unflagging childish smile on her face made up for it though.

"Are you sure you don't want to jump in the pool?"

"Later."

"Really?"

As I watched her go up and down, on that summer afternoon as warm as all the summer afternoons when I had failed before, I started turning a strange idea over in my mind. I ended up deciding there and then, both on Rosana's behalf and to give myself the sensation of breaking something: "When we come back later I'm going to go up on the highest board and dive off."

"That board's really very high."

"If I crack my head open on the bottom of the pool you can slip away quietly. Just catch a bus and don't tell anybody anything. They'll take care of burying me, you needn't worry about that."

"I don't want you to dive, Jaime."

Rosana seemed genuinely worried. We went back to where we'd left our things and she barely spoke for the next half hour. The sun was going down and the people who'd arrived in the morning were beginning to leave. Before my resolution could falter, I took my T-shirt off and suggested to Rosana that we went back to the pool.

"Don't do it, I mean it," she insisted.

"It's okay. I've done it loads of times."

Five minutes later I was more than fifteen feet above the water, looking back over my life. It was a lovely afternoon, a cool breeze was blowing and there were hardly any swimmers in the pool. I thought again about the speed at which I would hit the water, the braking power of its liquid mass and the depth of the pool. In my case, the diver's skill was completely irrelevant. Rosana was waiting on the pool side. I saw someone walk up to her from behind and start talking to her. A young Richard Gere lookalike, same mane of hair, more or less same complexion. Rosana turned to face him and at that moment someone in my head shouted *banzai* and I found myself flying straight toward the bottom of the abyss. I only just had time to tense my body and press my legs together. A moron who dies plunging off a diving board is pathetic, but a moron who dies plunging off a diving board and falls with his legs all over the place is verging on the grotesque.

The water hit my head as if I'd smacked it on an awning. Then the awning tore and I went further and further down in the middle of a bubbling whirlwind. I didn't put up any resistance, it even seemed undignified to resist, but suddenly my neck twisted upwards like a spring and something grazed my knee and the big toe of my left foot started stinging. I was safe and sound and the only way was up. I don't have the patience to commit suicide by drowning.

The ascent seemed interminable, although it could have gone on for ages, which is how long the air in my lungs would have lasted. When my head broke the surface I couldn't see anything. I ducked back under and swam underwater over to the ladder. I put my feet on the rungs, grabbed the rails and dragged myself out of the water. Above me, lighting up the sunset with her blue eyes, was Rosana.

"You're a liar. That's the first time you've done it" she scolded me.

"How did you guess?"

"Nobody who knows what they're doing dives like that. You're crazy."

Rosana reached out her hand and brushed the damp fringe off my forehead. She didn't do anything, she just looked at me and I saw that her pupils were larger than those of any other girl who had looked at me on the side of a swimming pool in the twilight. Perhaps I should have reproached myself for having plunged off the diving board, or Rosana for being impressed, but I preferred to interpret that a bit differently, that it wasn't my jump that had impressed her, but the fact I had done it without knowing how.

When happiness is too complete, when you're cured of truly horrific injury, when everything is too beautiful, there is only one feeling a sensible man can have: something is about to go completely fucking wrong. I had this premonition at that moment, while Rosana loved me and I was aware of it, and so I sank into the melancholy that I haven't been able to shed since then.

When we left the swimming pool parking lot in my cousin's car, I was overwhelmed by the sensation of having left behind whatever it was that justified that afternoon. One of the few ways of getting through life is thinking about something we want that's going to happen to us. When it finally happens, and you always realize when it does even if you didn't have a clear idea of what exactly you were longing for, the whole house of cards collapses. As anyone who hasn't yet taken up the modern habit of not reflecting on the essentials knows, what's important is not your wish coming true, but the fact that it hasn't done so yet and the possibility that it will.

As I accelerated with my good foot and controlled the clutch with my bad foot, which I had scraped on the bottom of the pool, I came to the conclusion that I had no choice but to return Rosana to her parents and forget about this game. After rummaging amongst my worse inclinations, I realized that I lacked the nerve to go beyond the point I had reached. My scruples were, in part, what held me back. Some of my colleagues had daughters Rosana's age, and some of them were guys I more or less respected. They would have despised me for my behavior and it bothered me that I had no arguments of substance to defend myself against that kind of scorn. Of course Rosana didn't exactly come across as a helpless little girl, but that could just have been a twisted evaluation on my part. And even if I needed to settle a score with fifteen year-old girls, such a need was an anomaly and I couldn't hope that anyone would understand it.

I was also afraid of the practical consequences. Of course, those that might be the result of the worst possible scenario—being discovered and having to answer for my dirty tricks before a judge—appalled me. But I was also haunted by a less serious and highly predictable outcome: that Rosana would suddenly become a woman within her teenage body and would stop being nice to me and even lose her looks and start to judge me. A man can free himself from a real woman using various widely recognised tactics that are easily put into practice. Many of these methods are even compatible with living under the same roof. On the other hand, there is no certain or easy way to free oneself from a woman-child, especially one with whom you're involved in an indecent relationship.

I was about to state aloud, and in slightly more heroic terms, my decision that we shouldn't see each other again, when Rosana had that idea she should never have had: "Let's go somewhere where there's nobody else around."

The sensible thing would have been for me not to give in to her whim. At some point I would have to put a stop to things and that was as good as any. However, I chose to persuade myself that doing what she wanted could buy me some time to find a clever way of convincing her.

“Of course, your wish is my command. Do you have somewhere in mind?” I asked.

“Somewhere around here. Somewhere you know.”

I racked my brain and finally remembered the vacant lot next to the Distance University building. I used to go there often when I was a student. I’d taken girls there before. I’d even broken up with a girlfriend there, in case the precedent was of any use. Once we arrived I drove over to a remote area, beneath some trees. I switched off the ignition and felt I had to be the first to speak.

“Rosana.”

“Yes.”

“You see,” I stammered, “sometimes you can’t do exactly what you want.”

“Right.”

“What I mean is, sometimes, however much you want something, you just have to let go.”

“What a shame.”

“Lots of things start out as jokes, and while something’s still a joke it doesn’t matter. But it can’t always be a joke. In the end things take a serious turn and you have to be more careful.”

“I thought you were going to kiss me.”

“What?”

Rosana drew closer. She had turned voluptuous and it was hard for me to get used to seeing her like that.

“I’m afraid you won’t be the first,” she said, and it was as if she suddenly was twenty years older. “Not in this, nor the rest.”

“I can see it’s pointless trying to explain this to you,” I squirmed. “I’m not going to be anything with you. Let’s go.”

I can't swear that I would've kept my word if I'd had to resist her incitement for any length of time. But there was no more time. Before my hand could touch the key to start the ignition, the car doors opened and someone lifted me out of my seat as if I were nothing more than a teddy bear stuffed with foam rubber.

On occasion, and fortunately these are few and far between, you look round and realize that hell, the wrath of God and rotten luck really do exist and not only can they catch up with you, but they do. In the movies, Evil is normally represented as something more or less monstrous that crushes you mercifully quickly. In reality, Evil is human and much slower. That afternoon for example, it came disguised as three individuals who must have been just over twenty years old. One had a shaved head and was about two metres tall, the second one had long, dishevelled hair and was wearing an enormous spiked wristband, the last, who seemed to be in charge, was unremarkable as regards his hair, and was wearing army boots.

It was the skinhead who had dragged me out of the car. After lifting me clean into the air he stood me on the ground and made sure I couldn't move by twisting my arm behind my back and crushing my neck with his forearm, which was significantly thicker than my torso and about thirty times as hard. For one stupid moment, the only thing that crossed my mind was that I hadn't expected the regression to childhood I'd feared when I agreed to go to the swimming pool with Rosana would be quite so complete. Then I was scared, shit scared. The guy with the matted hair had grabbed Rosana and had his hand clamped over her mouth. He had to because she was trying to shout.

"Tell the little bitch to shut her trap, boss, or Yoni will split her head open," the guy with the boots threatened me.

"Don't worry, Rosana, nothing's going to happen to you," I stuttered with difficulty.

"That's right, Rosana, nothing's going to happen to you, sweetie-pie," the ringleader reassured her.

The girl stopped struggling but Yoni didn't uncover her mouth. Given our situation, I hastened to bet, with little confidence, that this was not of prime importance.

"All my money's in the car, in the bag. There's about twenty thousand pesetas and my credit cards. I'll give you the pin number. It's nine zero ninety-nine for all of them."

"Very good, boss, you made the right move there."

"I bet that's the wrong code, Fredi," surmised Yoni, gratuitously and mistakenly.

"I'll put the squeeze on him a bit to check if you want," offered the guy with the shaved head.

"Wait, Urko, let me have a look," ordered Fredi. He got into the car and pulled out the bag. He found my wallet, counted the money and took out the cards.

"Nineteen grand, a Visa Gold card and three other less common ones. You're telling the truth boss, I'm sure the code's correct. Or is it? Let him have it, Urko."

Urko twisted my arm so hard I thought he was going to pull it off.

"I swear that's the code," I shouted.

"Enough, Urko. I believe him. In any case, we'll take him with us and if he's lying we'll beat the shit out of him. That way you can't cancel them either, eh chief? Now, let's have a look at the slut. You gonna give her to me too, boss?"

"Leave her alone, fuck it, she's just a kid," I begged.

"What?"

"Leave her alone. You've got a truckload of cash. You can get fifty thousand with each card, and you can buy yourselves a real broad each."

"I didn't catch that, boss. Did you say something?"

I swallowed. Everything was about to fucking explode and I had to take a risk, or rather, divert the problem onto myself.

"She hasn't done anything to you. If you touch her you're a fucking piece of shit."

"Boss you've had it! Hold him, Urko."

Fredi took a run up and, obviously, dealt me a kick in the soul, or rather, in my groin. Looking back, I think it's the first time I'd ever been kicked there, and it hurt so much that I have no words to describe it. I was left dangling from Urko's iron forearm, moaning and feeling the tears streaming down my face.

When I was able to open my eyes again, I saw Rosana, terrified and immobile. She no longer even seemed capable of shouting.

"I don't know what an old guy like you is doing with a little whore like her," Fredi pondered aloud, with exaggerated gestures. "And I've no idea how come she's such a good-looking little thing. What I do know is that she's for free and your cash will buy us a few drinks later. Hold her still, Yoni."

Rosana tried to shake them off but they had a good grip on her. Fredi pulled up her dress and ripped her panties off.

"I'll have these as a souvenir," he told me, squirrelling them away.

Hell, my personal hell, was that it was Fredi who revealed to me as night fell on that vacant lot, the treasure hiding under Rosana's dress. In my most abject moments, I had dreamed of doing it myself, but slowly and with a tenderness that Fredi didn't need and that now made me disgusted and full of self-loathing. Nor could I fail to acknowledge, in the midst of the horror, the tender beauty that was about to be devastated. Sinking right down to the depths of depravity, I have to confess I tried not to miss a single detail, because probably this would be the last instance of female nudity my eyes would see. In a fit of pride or rage I tried to free myself from Urko's grasp. My rebellion didn't last long. The giant squeezed my neck until I started to choke and could no longer struggle.

Fredi leant over Rosana to examine her. He turned to face me and bellowed, "This one's for you, boss."

Taking advantage of the other guy's distraction, the girl kneed him right on the nose. Fredi recoiled and almost fell over. When he regained his balance he put his hand up to his nose and brought it away wet with blood.

"Let her go, Yoni, for fuck's sake."

Yoni obeyed. Rosana found herself free and didn't understand what was happening until Fredi threw himself at her.

"If you want me to hurt you, I will, you little slut."

Then she looked at me, trying to hold onto something, didn't find anything and, sobbing, shouted, "Jaime."

Fredi charged on her like a rhinoceros. Rosana was thrown backwards, stumbled and fell on her back to the ground. I stared at the movement described by her head: when Fredi pushed her it jolted forwards, when she lost her balance it was thrown backwards, it jerked forward again before her back hit the ground then finally snapped back with a sound like someone cracking a nut and Rosana stopped moving.

Fredi didn't realize until he'd sat astride her and punched her on her face half a dozen times.

"Shit, you've killed her," murmured Urko behind me.

"Now you've really screwed us," agreed Yoni, half hysterical.

Incredulous, Fredi stared down at the body he was sitting on.

"Now what?" Yoni shouted at him.

Fredi was still staring blankly. Urko relaxed his iron grip.

"For fuck's sake. You can wait here for the cops to come, you dick," said Yoni and he ran off.

Fredi watched him go and then stared once again at the body. Without taking his eyes off her he ordered Urko, "Kill him. If he opens his mouth we'll be rotting in prison till we die."

Urko let me go.

"You're nuts, Fredi. This is your mess and I'm not digging myself in deeper to help you. The fucking bitch was just a kid. The guy was right. We could have gone and found ourselves some real broads."

"It's our mess, all of us" said Fredi, getting up. "And we'll catch up with Yoni, piece of shit he turned out to be. But you're okay, Urko. Don't start spouting this now. Grab him."

The giant stepped between us.

"I'm getting the hell out of here," he announced firmly, "and so are you. If they catch us, what happened to the broad was an accident and it was your fault. If we kill the old guy, it's murder, man. Then they'll send us down for sure."

"Get out of the way. If you haven't got the balls, I'll do it."

Urko didn't give him the chance to say another word. He punched him in the stomach and in the face, smashing it in. But he held onto him to make sure he didn't hurt himself in his fall. Then he slung him over his shoulder. Before he left he gave me back my wallet and said, "Take it. If the pigs implicate me, remember what I did for you. I'm sorry, man."

Urko started running and I stood there, stunned, a few feet from Rosana's lifeless body. It took me a few seconds to get close to it. I knelt down next to her, pulled her dress down so it covered her and stroked her soft, blonde hair. Her eyes were closed. Some idiot might think it was better she died before that lowlife dishonoured her. And perhaps I'm that idiot, but I would have given anything for her to open her eyes or to hear her voice again.

One of the things the police inspector has asked me most often, because apparently it's the weakest point in my "story", as he calls it, is why, instead of calling the police, I got into my car and drove off, leaving Rosana lying there until a student out jogging found her the next morning. It's not something I fully understand myself. On the one hand, it's not so strange that a man who hangs out with a fifteen-year-old girl and takes her to a place like that and then has the misfortune of watching her get killed can't bring himself to call the police. But what disturbed me above all was that last word coming from Rosana's mouth, my assumed name sobbed like a prayer that couldn't prevent anything of what was hovering over her. I had taken Rosana out of her danger-free world, I had taken her as if she were mine and she had paid with her life for trying to please me. Even though I couldn't think straight at the time, I think I fled precisely so that they would accuse me, because I considered or consider myself to be as guilty as, or guiltier than, the despicable rat who broke her neck. Ever since that night, Rosana turns up in all my nightmares, sobbing my assumed name until I wake up trembling with my heart in my mouth.

They will sentence me one day, I suppose, and it's possible that when I resign myself to deserving it I'll find peace. She will come at night, when I am expecting the arrival of the nightmare my faults earned me, and suddenly she will be the happy, mysterious Rosana of our first meeting, brushing the fringe off my forehead while her pupils dilate and flood her blue gaze. She will smile and she will say my real name, the one I always hid from her, and so, in the end, the filthy Bolshevik will know that the young Grand Duchess has pardoned him.

Shortly after leaving the vacant lot I found myself on the motorway to La Coruña. Due to the state of shock I was in, I had taken the road for La Coruña instead of the one to Madrid. I remembered that I'd got my money and cards back and so I didn't turn around.

I drove all night. I stopped to refuel in the middle of the Castilian tableland, I couldn't say exactly where. I drove the rest of the way to La Coruña without stopping, and since it was still very early in the morning when I got there I took the road to Cape Finisterre. Dawn found me on the cliffs, leaning against the car, waiting at the mercy of the breeze.

Whenever I've driven somewhere, once I've covered sufficient distance to feel far away from home, I've always enjoyed getting out of the car, leaning on it and looking at the countryside, the sea or whatever's there in front of me. There's something comforting in the solitude you experience, your own and that of the car that is subject to your will, with no option but to go and take you wherever you drive it, even if you accelerate just for the sake of accelerating, with no fixed destination in mind.

That morning, facing the end of the earth over which I had driven all night, the solitude was so great and my disorientation so absolute that I forgot the time. I was there for hours, and before I left something happened that I can't help pointing out. My eyes suddenly filled with tears and a shiver went down my spine. It was then that I realized, as perhaps I hadn't realized for the last ten years, that I was alive, and in the middle of the catastrophe I gave thanks for being alive, and not lying dead in the middle of a vacant lot like Rosana. Nobody would take my side, I could already imagine how even I would torture myself, and on noticing what was running through my head I considered myself as much a son of a bitch as anyone reading this now will. In spite of this, I gave thanks, and accepted that I was indebted to Rosana for my good luck and her misfortune.

From that morning on, I had the task of bringing something of her into all the mornings she would never see again. For this reason, although my lawyer says it won't support my presumption of innocence, I cut out all the photographs of Rosana that have been published in the press and I've built a sort of little altar before which I meditate for ten minutes every morning while listening to the first movement of *Der Tod und das Mädchen*. When the string quartet reaches the highest point of this divine melody that the world owes to Franz Schubert, I remember how she used to laugh, how she used to walk and also, why not, how stunning she looked in that pink bikini.

It took them almost two weeks to turn up at my apartment to arrest me. The investigation was thorough rather than lengthy. The obscene or simply bizarre phone calls to the López-Díaz household were immediately linked with Rosana's sad end, plainly a maniac's doing. The police found my stupid conversation with Rosana's mother on the eve of the event particularly illuminating. The girl's presence at a swimming pool on the afternoon of the crime with a man in his thirties was also quickly established. Barely a couple of days later, it was confirmed, thanks to Izaskun and the other girls, that a man in his thirties had been prowling around the school. With a bit more effort, various witnesses of our meetings in the Retiro park appeared. Naturally I'm dispensing with all the false leads, from those who'd seen Rosana dancing with a legionnaire in a Torremolinos disco the night before to the person who swore they'd seen her being forced to sell herself at roadside dive near Cuenca. The strange thing about this false lead, and the reason I remember it, is that the young girl who had caused the misunderstanding was freed by the police afterwards and it turned out that she was a Russian named Olga Nikolayevna who'd been illegally trafficked from her country.

Since I had no criminal record, the investigation came up against the stumbling block that none of the witnesses recognised me among the maniacs they had on file. But a competent female inspector interviewed the family extensively until Sonsoles remembered she'd been involved in a road accident the day the unexplained calls started. They got my name from the insurance company and then the pictures and all the witnesses started pointing the finger of blame at me and from that point I could consider myself screwed.

The day they nabbed me, while they were handcuffing me and reading me my rights, the inspector responsible for my arrest looked at me with such hatred and satisfaction that I had to reconsider the strange fact that Evil can also nestle in the generous bosom of the Good. And in the car the inspector put her feelings into words, "I know that seat has a a lot to tell, but I doubt it's ever had a piece of shit like you sitting on it."

In one way I agreed with her. However, I took her to task for being so vicious: "'For with what judgment you judge, you will be judged; and with the measure you use, it will be measured back to you.' Gospel of Matthew, chapter seven, verse two."

"I couldn't give a fuck. I'm an atheist."

"Not a very prudent religious option, but I respect it. What do you give a fuck about, if you don't mind my asking?"

According to my lawyer, who seems to be a pretty meticulous young lady, it would have been better to keep that question to myself.

One afternoon when I was halfway through the notebook, I began to think about how the story would end. These are some of the possible endings: offer up some cautionary moral message for those youngsters still on the straight and narrow; beg for clemency; describe Fredi and Urko in great detail in case they were caught committing some other violent crime one day; say to hell with it all and give a raw account of my most pornographic fantasy about Rosana. After carefully weighing up all the options, I decided I would write something contrary to my convictions.

Convictions are highly valued today, I suspect due to the general guilty conscience that there are so few of them and they are so basic. However, you can never be sure what good any conviction might do, nor where it came from. Now is the time for me to declare that convictions usually have dubious origins and absurd intentions, and that a lot of effort is wasted as a result of them, and cruel suffering inflicted on innocent people. For that reason it's a good idea from time to time to try maintaining the opposite to what you believe and to find out whether it can be even more convincing than your own belief. Then you can go back to your starting point, because the important thing is not to be right, but to feel good. In the same vein, if the opposite stance to your conviction makes you feel more at ease, whether or not it's more persuasive than your conviction, there's no sensible option but to change your position. Growing bitter due to a chance loyalty is a sign of immaturity.

My nature is not well disposed to conviction. Almost everything I've seen has taught me to be quite sceptical. However, it's undeniable that even an unbeliever finds certain bastard forms of conviction in that same unbelief. In the course of these pages I've gradually revealed a few, but there's a specific one that I would now like to refute as I say my farewells: that you should ignore your fellow men and that devotion to another person brings about the self-destruction of whoever practices it.

The facts are that, soon after discovering her, while rummaging freely in her sister's life, I allowed myself to get close to a beautiful young girl I didn't know, and I did so in a state of blind rapture. It is also true that as a direct consequence of that action, more than any unpredictable misfortune, my life has been ruined, probably forever. I've lost my job, my good name, my freedom and all my credit cards. They've also seized my car and I've experienced various new and extreme forms of pain. In short, the facts seem to uphold my original conviction. What could go against that?

I've come here tonight to say goodbye and to maintain that a man is no more than the pieces of himself he's given up in sacrifice for others. Everything he suffers on his own account is shit that falls in the barren desert. What one suffers for another human being, on the other hand, is the seed from which springs the tree of memory. And that tree protects man from the threat of the desert sand and shit, from oblivion and death.

Before my downfall took on the specific shape of Rosana, I was nothing, I was a nobody. The days used to wash over me like waves on a deserted beach. Trapped between my sarcasm and my mood swings, I fought my way through life without enjoyment or surprise. And the fact is that, almost by definition, a person can't do anything decisive for themself (I include the word *decisive* to exclude trivial self-serving things that don't have anything to do with this: brushing one's teeth, cutting one's nails, feeding oneself, switching the television off). It's also true that you can't do anything decisive for other people and that other people can't do anything decisive for you. What I learned thanks to Rosana was that only when you think about someone else, and only in this way, can you really accomplish something decisive for yourself.

One summer afternoon I abandoned everything to make Rosana the main purpose of my existence. Maybe at times my intentions have been frivolous, this deserves the reproach it deserves, but it doesn't erase the fact that she became the axis around which everything began to orbit. Then, almost immediately, she disappeared and I was left with just her memory and a sense of longing, and ever since the sense of longing and her memory are, more or less, the only things that concern me since then. I've stopped worrying about what might become of me, what I am, was or could have been. I no longer feel sorry for myself, because I have no sadness left after using it all up on her absence. Since I met her, and most of all ever since she left, there's been no room for anything else but her in either my soul or brain.

Now the rabble insults me, mothers use my name to threaten little girls who won't eat their food, and if I were in Arkansas my lawyer would be appealing, without much hope, for me to be spared the electric chair. And it's now, only now, that for the first time in my life I have the impression of having been something. Before, if God had asked me what I'd done with the time he'd allotted me, I would only have been able to offer him a miserable inventory list of my entire history. Today it would be different. If he came today to call me to account, I would first confess that I have sinned, often and grievously. Then I would unroll the parchment of my memory and say, "I have not been impious. I have longed for the light of your angels, I managed to brush against it and in the end I ruined it. I was guilty, although it wasn't intentional. I have spent the rest of my life as follows: before then, waiting for her; afterwards, paying for it."

Apart from Thomas Aquinas, who had the arrogance to demonstrate Him several times and in different ways, nobody has a concrete idea of who God is or what he's like. Personally, something I've always suspected, and it's a wager like any other, is that He is a fan of symmetry and an enemy of the incomplete. That is why I maintain a timid belief that when I show him my wares, He will condescend to offer me reasonable reward.

I beg anyone who may be in a position to exercise any influence to intercede in favor of this to grant me one humble request: the next time I meet Rosana, may we both be fifteen, may I not be a Bolshevik (whether or not she's a Grand Duchess is neither here nor there) and may someone keep that son of a bitch Fredi and the rest of his ilk out of the story.

Madrid-Getafe-Dublin
27 March-11 July 1995

ABOUT THE AUTHOR

Lorenzo Silva is one of the leading writers of his generation, best known for his five detective novels *El lejano país de los estanques* (The Far Away Pond Land), *El alquimista impaciente* (The Impatient Alchemist), *La niebla y la doncella* (The Mist and the Maiden), *La reina sin espejo* (The Queen Without a Mirror), and *La estrategia del agua* (Water's Stategy), all published by Destino, and all featuring the detective Rubén Bevilacqua and his young assistant Virginia Chamorro, who together represent the new face of Spain's Guardia Civil—a very different animal from its infamous predecessors. While already brilliant in themselves, Silva's stories are enhanced by the subplots the author weaves into the relationship between Bevilacqua and Chamorro, which become as riveting as the main plot, and the snappy dialogue adds to the sheer delight of reading these novels. Silva is a sensitive and intelligent voice for our time, whose other works include *The Fainthearted Bolshevik*, *El nombre de los nuestros* (The Name of our People), *La sustancia interior* (The Inner Substance), *El blog del inquisidor* (The Inquisitor's Blog), *Carta Blanca* (Carte Blanche) and *Niños feroces* (Fierce Children), as well as books for young adults and children. He has won the Ojo Crítico Award (1998), the Nadal Award (2000) and the Primavera Award (2004) and his latest novel, *La marca del meridiano,* won the Planeta Award in 2012, one of the best known Spanish literary prizes.

www.lorenzo-silva.com

ABOUT THE TRANSLATORS

NICK CAISTOR is an English translator of fiction from Spanish, French, and Portuguese. He worked for many years as a BBC Latin American analyst, and has translated more than 35 books from Latin America and Spain, including authors such as Juan Carlos Onetti, Alan Pauls, Andrés Neuman, and Eduardo Mendoza, Juan Marsé and Manuel Vázquez Montalbán. He has twice been awarded the Valle-Inclán prize for translations from Spanish.

ISABELLE KAUFELER studied Spanish and Italian at Cambridge University and has a Masters in Literary Translation from the University of East Anglia, where she was on the editorial team for the *Norwich Papers* translation journal. She has also attended Spanish and Italian translation summer school workshops and reads for New Spanish Books. Previous projects include co-translations from Spanish with Nick Caistor and Michele Giuttari's *The Dark Heart of Florence* with Howard Curtis. She is currently translating a Spanish crime fiction novel.